THE CAIN CONSPIRACY

THE CAIN CONSPIRACY

THE CAIN SERIES BOOK 1

MIKE RYAN

WWW.MIKERYANBOOKS.COM

Copyright © 2016 by Mike Ryan

All rights reserved.

No part of this book may be reproduced in any form or by any electronic or mechanical means, including information storage and retrieval systems, without written permission from the author, except for the use of brief quotations in a book review.

Cover Design: Melody Simmons

1

Syria—Two U.S. citizens were captured and being held hostage in the basement of a Syrian house in the city of Al Qutayfa. They were part of a 23-member United Nations peacekeeping force who were monitoring events in the Golan Heights area between Israel and Syria. The other hostages had already been released and negotiations with the U.S. for the safe return of the Americans had broken down. The U.S. government decided the best course of action was to send in a small, elite team of soldiers to find the hostages and bring them back home. The U.S. Ambassador set up a meeting with Syrian officials for the following week to talk about freeing the hostages knowing that it would never take place. With luck, the team of soldiers would bring the prisoners back before then. The plan was set into action for the following night.

A ten-man force of Team Delta soldiers slipped into Syrian territory using the Lebanon border to enter. Lebanese officials were appraised of the action and were completely cooperating with the mission. The Lebanese government was happy to help as they had their own issues with Syria. All entries between the two countries had been closed due to feuding and policy differences. Lebanon agreed to also let the U.S. use its airspace for the mission's conclusion. Black Hawk helicopters from the 160th SOAR would bring the team and its evacuees to safety into Lebanese territory before heading to their base in Israel. The Night Stalkers, as they're frequently called, are often used on missions conducted at night and at high speeds. Al Qutayfa was less than 50 miles from the Lebanese border, so a small band of soldiers could still reach the city on foot in a relatively quick period of time. It would also be close enough for them to evacuate on the Black Hawk and be out of Syria within minutes. The team had to be on guard for not only Syrian forces, but also rebels. It was possible for Syrian forces to be on one street and rebels on the next street over. Both were equally dangerous to the squad.

    The Delta team was led by Captain Terry. He had led several rescue missions before and had been on the ground in Syria previously. An informant had given the tip about the location of the U.S. prisoners, and a picture taken with a cell phone was used as proof that they were still alive. They appeared to have some cuts on their faces so it was assumed they'd been beaten. There was no telling how much more time they had until they met their end, so the mission needed to take place now. They were being held in the basement of a four-story residence on the edge of the city. If there was a positive, it was that they wouldn't have to fight their way out of the entire city.

    The squad reached the outskirts of the city by nightfall. They took cover amongst a clump of trees that were on the other side of the road that led into the city. There wasn't much activity on the roads, but enough for the team to stay undercover as they waited a little while longer. They identified their target location as the informant marked the side of the building with black chalk. It was a rather plain looking building. Tan in color, there were four stories, with lots of windows and balconies. As soon as traffic slowed down a little more, they'd make their move on the residence. While they waited, Terry went over the plan with his men one more time. Once they breached the building seven of the men would go inside to rescue the hostages while three would remain outside. Two would protect each corner of the building and the other would watch the door to make sure the backs of the other two soldiers were protected. As he finished up, Terry's radio started.

"Romeo Two-Four to Echo One-Two, come in."

"This is Echo One-Two, over," Terry responded.

"What is your status, over?"

"We are just outside the target location. Waiting for activity to die down a little, over."

"Roger that. Let us know when you begin your approach so we can get Super Six-Two en route."

"Roger that."

Captain Terry continued talking to his men to make sure there was no confusion about anything. "Everyone remember the rules of engagement; nobody fires unless fired upon. We don't know how many people are in that building, so be alert."

The mission required precise planning and timing. Once Black Hawk Super Six-Two entered Syrian airspace, it could possibly be subject to air defense missiles. Israel became involved in the mission at the request of the U.S. government. Israel had previously been successful at confusing Syria's air defense system by using an array of intense electronic warfare operations to confuse and deceive Syrian communications. They were able to successfully block Syrian radar units to where they could not detect an enemy presence in their skies. Israel would attempt to do the same to protect their U.S. counterparts but could not guarantee the same results. Therefore, the ground team needed to radio Super Six-Two when they were ready to be picked up so they could arrive at the exact time needed. Any delay by the ground team or the Black Hawk would compromise everyone involved. A couple of hours passed and Captain Terry waited until midnight before beginning their approach. The road was virtually deserted and hadn't had any traffic on it for over an hour. He contacted JSOC in Israel to inform them.

"Romeo Two-Four, this is Echo One-Two. We're beginning our approach now, over," Terry said.

"Roger, Echo One-Two."

The Delta team emerged from the cover of the trees and quickly ran across the highway. They encountered no resistance and reached their target location without incident. There was a small fence surrounding the development, but it had numerous holes in it so the team had no problem getting through. It looked like the complex was going through some renovations as there was a small ditch in back of the property that ran the length of the building with some construction material along the fence. The soldiers took up residence in the ditch for a

The Cain Conspiracy

minute as they sized up the situation. Three men stayed in their positions in the ditch to cover their respective areas as the rest of the team approached the door. Captain Terry quietly turned the handle to see if it was open. He shook his head to the rest of the group to indicate it wasn't. It was a plain wooden door which wouldn't take much to break down. Terry stepped aside as another man stepped up with his size eleven boots and kicked the door open on the first try. The group quickly entered with their M4A1 carbines raised, ready to fire. They hoped it would be a mission where they could quickly identify the prisoners and get them out before anyone knew they were there, without an eruption of gunfire. This, however, would not be one of those missions. As soon as the Delta team breached the door, four men seated at a square wooden table jumped up with their weapons drawn. They were immediately taken down with a barrage of bullets. There were two more in the corner of the room that were dispersed of before they had a chance to reach their assault rifles.

"Nails, stairs," Terry yelled at one of the soldiers.

"Got it," he replied.

Nails was probably the most respected man of the unit. He was a ten-year soldier and was often picked for the toughest assignments. He was nicknamed Nails by his fellow soldiers for being as "tough as nails." He never complained about anything and just did his job as well as he could. Everyone respected him for it. Nails had his eyes, and his M4 locked on the stairs to the side of the room in case any of the insurgents came rushing down the steps. A few seconds later he had a couple targets in his crosshairs as two men came running down, only to be cut in half as they fell down the steps. The rest of the team carefully reached the basement steps and began descending them. It was pitch dark in the basement, though the Delta members could see with their night vision goggles on. As soon as they reached halfway down the steps, gunfire screamed out, and three soldiers jumped down the steps, diving onto the floor, ready to fire. The other three halted, and retreated up the steps. There were some barrels on the far side of the basement. It seemed to be the only spot for someone to take cover. Didn't take long to find out as a couple heads peeked over the barrels seconds later. The prisoners were tied together along the side of one of the walls so they were sure it wasn't them peeking over. The soldiers waited for the insurgents to fire so they could be sure of what they were hitting. There was a small piece of wood by Terry's hand that he picked up and tossed across the room, away from the prisoners. The noise drew the fire of the insurgents, which immediately caused the soldiers to fire in their direction. The two men fell into the barrels, knocking them over, as the men lay on the floor, bleeding out.

"Shit," Terry stated, as he heard gunfire erupting outside the building. He grabbed his radio to bring in the Black Hawk. "Echo One-Two to Super Six-Two, over."

"This is Super Six-Two, over."

"Prisoners secured, Six-Two. We're coming out now."

"Roger One-Two, we're on route. ETA ten minutes."

"Roger that."

The prisoners were quickly untied and asked a couple questions to make sure they were who they were supposed to be. Although their faces had taken a little pounding, they weren't in such bad shape that they couldn't walk, which would make the escape much easier. The group rushed up the steps where Nails was still holding down the steps.

"Sounds like trouble outside," Nails said.

The men outside found their own problems as a group of rebels heard the gunfire and rushed over to see what it was. The two soldiers on the corners were holding down their spots without much problem.

"Coming out," Terry yelled.

"You're clear," the soldier watching the door shouted.

The group came out, Nails guarding behind them.

"We've got ten minutes," Terry informed the group. "Let's move out."

As soon as they began to move, Nails started firing back into the building as insurgents came running down the steps. They got to the fence while still guarding their backs and one by one went through the hole. They were met with gunfire on the other side, though, as a group of rebels took position down the road. The team waited a minute as they figured out the best option. They had to move soon as more rebels were starting to flank them.

"Sir, we need to move," Nails yelled. "Starting to get hot back here."

Terry and two other soldiers started firing at the rebels on the road to provide a little cover for the rest of the team to cross the road as Nails kept firing towards the complex. Nails started to cross when he suddenly dropped to the ground. Terry looked behind him and noticed that Nails wasn't moving. He ran toward him and knelt down at his side. Nails was still breathing though it was heavy, and he appeared to be unconscious. Terry moved Nails' head and noticed the hole in his forehead. Terry and another man dragged him the rest of the way as the rest of the group unleashed a barrage of gunfire toward the insurgents.

"Super Six-Two this is Echo One-Two, we got a hornet's nest behind us, over," Terry quickly yelled.

"Roger Echo One-Two, we're comin' in hot and heavy," the pilot said.

"Roger that. We're putting smoke down just along the trees. Fire whatever you got north of that and it should give us a little more time."

"Roger One-Two. We got you covered."

Terry put down some green smoke to mark their positions so the Night Stalker could fire its machine guns on the enemy. Terry and his men continued through the trees as one of them carried Nails over his shoulder. Just as they reached the edge of the trees the Black Hawk came in as promised, firing its M240 machine gun just north of the green smoke rising through the air. A few rocket propelled grenades went scorching through the air, trying to take down the helicopter, though none hit their intended target. The rebels had no choice but to retreat or else they risked being cut to shreds by the Black Hawk. The Night Stalker then set itself down just beyond the trees as the Delta team rushed toward it. Once they all safely boarded, the helicopter was up in the air. The Israelis had successfully blocked the air missiles of the Syrian army so the helicopter was never in danger and didn't even appear on their radar. As the Black Hawk flew back to base, Terry took a few deep breaths and made sure the rest of his men were OK. A couple had minor bumps and bruises, but none sustained any major injuries, except for Nails.

"Romeo Two-Four to Echo One-Two, come in," the radio bellowed.

"This is Echo One-Two, over," Terry replied.

"Roger One-Two, what's your status?"

"We have one man critical and have both prisoners in tow. Will need immediate medical attention as soon as we touch down."

"Roger that."

2

New York—Director Ed Sanders was concluding a meeting with his deputy directors when a call came in on the intercom.

"Director Sanders, sir?"

"Yes, go ahead."

"We've just learned of a situation in Syria. The possibility exists for a new recruit."

"Excellent. We're done here. Bring the information in," Sanders said.

A man came in, file folder in hand, and walked around the oval table where the seven men were seated. He handed the folder to Sanders, who immediately began looking over its contents.

"So, what do we have here?" Sanders asked.

"A soldier with Team Delta is in critical condition in a combat support hospital in Israel. He was shot in the head while on a mission in Syria."

"And what are his prospects?"

"Actually, pretty good. He just came out of surgery

The Cain Conspiracy

about 30 minutes ago and is in stable condition. The bullet's been removed and they think he's gonna make it," the officer informed the staff. "His military record makes him an ideal candidate."

"Excellent. Get the jet ready for Israel," Sanders told his subordinate as he stood up. "Gentlemen, we'll convene next week as usual."

Sanders gathered a few things and called for his car to be ready. He summoned for a few operators to meet him. He made his way down to the basement where his car was waiting for him. He got in the back seat and began reading the background of the soldier he was about to meet. His military records, as well as his personal transcripts, went as far back as elementary school.

"What's the verdict, sir?" his lieutenant asked.

"There are some issues which we'll have to overcome. But nothing's ever perfect. I think he should do nicely," Sanders responded.

∽

Israel Combat Support Hospital—The four government officials stepped into the hospital and were immediately taken to the commander, Colonel Jefferson.

"Can I help you, gentlemen?" Jefferson asked.

"We'd like to know all you can tell us about this man," Sanders said, handing the colonel a paper with the soldier's name on it.

"I'm not at liberty to discuss anything with you."

"I believe you will," Sanders said, pulling out his top-secret clearance. "Unless you wanna take this matter to the very top and I don't think you do."

"He had surgery early this morning to remove a bullet in his head. The surgery was successful, and he's currently recovering."

"What are the chances that he actually makes it?"

"I'd say he's already done it. Gunshot wounds to the head are fatal about 90% of the time. The biggest issue is the loss of blood. Most die before they even reach a hospital. For those lucky enough to get to a hospital alive, 50% will die during the surgery. So, considering he's made it through the biggest two hurdles, I'd say his outlook is good," Jefferson said.

"Is he currently awake?"

"Not yet. He'll be kept under sedation for the next couple of days so we can monitor him for any swelling in the brain."

"What will his prognosis be?"

"Impossible to say at this point. If you want to say a man who's shot in the head is lucky, you can say he is. The brain has two hemispheres, each with four lobes, and in his case the bullet was only lodged in one hemisphere in a single lobe. It appears that a limited amount of tissue was damaged."

"How long will it take for him to recover?"

"It depends on his condition. If he wakes up and the damage is as minimal as we think it is, he could be up and about within a couple weeks. If there's further damage, it could take months or years. The major issues would be motor, sensory, cognition, memory, speech, and vision. Any combination of damage in these areas could set him back in his recovery. I should also note that 50% of people who survive will suffer from seizures and require anti-epilepsy medication."

"I thank you for all the information, Colonel. I'm going to leave two of my men here for a few days in case anything arises that needs my attention. They will stay out of your way and will stay with our subject to observe the entire time."

"I don't suppose I can say no," the Colonel noted.

"You could. Wouldn't do you any good though."

"I thought not."

"I expect your cooperation with anything my men need."

"They'll get it."

"I'll be back in a few days."

Sanders left instructions with the officers he was leaving behind to stay by the soldier's bed until he was awake. They left the hospital to go back to New York for a couple days, eager for the soldier's awakening. On the flight back, Sanders worked out some of the details for the inclusion of a new recruit to the organization.

Once back in New York, Sanders asked his secretary to get Michelle Lawson on the phone for him. Lawson was one of the organization's top handlers. She had previously worked with the FBI as a data information specialist. She quickly gained a reputation for being extremely smart and acquiring mounds of information almost instantly. That was one of the principal reasons why Sanders wanted her in his employment. Lawson had been able to garner the trust of every agent she ever worked with, for being able to get anything they needed and helped them out of tough predicaments when necessary. Though she didn't have movie star looks, more of the pretty girl next door, she was an attractive woman that never used her looks to her advantage. She was on the smaller side, about 5'3" and thin, with short, dirty blonde hair. Within minutes, Lawson was on the line.

"Shelly, how are you?" Sanders asked.

"I'm good, sir. Your secretary sounded like she was in a hurry so I figured something important was going on."

"It is. We may have a new recruit in a few days."

"That's great."

"I'm still working out the logistics of everything, but I was thinking of adding him to your team. Are you able to handle one more? How many agents are you handling right now?"

"Right now, I have seven agents. One more shouldn't be a problem," she said.

"Fantastic. Where are you right now?"

"I'm in Madrid. I was going over a mission with Agent Samson."

"How soon can you wrap things up there? When can you get back to New York?" Sanders wondered.

"I can wrap everything up here tomorrow and be there the day after."

"That's fine. I would like you to be here when we introduce him to everything and to get you acquainted."

"I look forward to it, sir."

"Great. I'll see you in a few days then."

"One more thing. What's his name?"

"I guess that might be useful, huh? His name... is Matthew Cain."

Two days later Sanders got the call from one of his liaison officers in Israel to update the injured soldier's condition. The doctors were no longer giving him sedatives and expected him to be alert the next day. Sanders immediately booked a flight for his private jet to leave for

Ben Gurion International Airport near Tel Aviv near midnight so he'd arrive the following morning. Once he and his staff landed, they promptly made their way to the hospital. They were greeted by his officers once they reached the hospital and went to Cain's bed.

"Has he been awake yet?"

"Not yet, sir, but they expect him to be pretty soon," an officer responded.

"OK. Except for Shelly, the rest of you clear out of here," Sanders told the bunch. "I don't wanna smother him with people the moment he wakes up."

Sanders and Lawson grabbed a couple of chairs and waited near the bed, pulling out their iPads to do some work while they marked time. They wouldn't have to wait long as the soldier woke up about an hour later. The government officials stayed out of the way as the doctors checked on him and made sure there were no complications. They were eager to finally talk to him and see the effects of the surgery. As the doctors were finishing up, Sanders stood at the end of the bed. He nodded at Lawson to follow the doctors out to speak with them.

"How are you feeling, soldier?" Sanders asked.

"Other than feeling like someone's using a sledgehammer on my head, I guess OK."

"Remember anything about what happened?"

The soldier lifted his head, slightly sitting up, and gazed down at the floor. A terrifying realization came over him as his mind was a complete blank. Sanders could tell by the concerned look that swept over his face that he was having trouble coming up with anything. The soldier ran his hand over his head, letting his fingers feel the stitches that permeated his skull.

"What's your name?" Sanders asked.

The soldier opened his mouth as if he was about to spit it out, but closed it a moment later, shaking his head in disgust.

"How long do I have to be in here?" the soldier asked.

"Doctors say a couple weeks, depending on how you do with everything," Sanders replied.

"You're not a doctor?"

"Don't really have the uniform for it," Sanders said, looking down at his black suit.

"Who are you?"

"Director Ed Sanders."

"Director of what?"

"Well, we'll get into that another time. The most important thing right now is you."

"I can't remember anything," the soldier said, frustration clearly evident in his voice.

"That might be the least of your worries. They'll be coming in here soon to test your other faculties."

Sanders started walking away toward Lawson, then stopped to look back at the soldier.

"By the way, your name is Thomas Nelson. You were a member of Delta Force on a special mission when you were shot in the head."

The doctors came back in and started talking to Nelson in more detail. Sanders took Lawson aside to make sure her discussion with the doctors was productive.

"Are they going to cooperate?" Sanders asked.

"They were a little hesitant at first, but I convinced them it was the best move they could make in the interest of national security. There'll be no problems," she replied.

"Excellent," Sanders said as his phone rang. "Stay in there with them to make sure there are no hiccups."

Sanders took his conversation outside to avoid any prying ears. Lawson went back to Nelson as the doctors were checking him out.

"How's he looking?" Lawson asked.

"Vitals are looking good," a doctor noted. "Just saw the MRI results. There's no bleeding, clots, or swelling. Some minor tissue damage but, all in all, everything's looking fantastic."

"That's great."

The doctor left the room and Nelson lay still, staring up at the ceiling, wondering when he was going to start remembering things.

"I take it you're not a doctor either?" Nelson asked, not bothering to look at his visitor.

"No, I'm not."

"You with the other guy?"

"If you're referring to Director Sanders, then yes, I am," she replied.

"What do you want?"

"In a few minutes, a specialist is going to come in here and give you a series of tests."

"What kind?"

"Just to see what kind of additional rehab, if any, you're going to need. I've already heard about your memory. We're going to need to see if you're having any other difficulties with your vision, motor skills, things like that."

"If you're not a doctor, then why are you here?" Nelson asked.

"We work for the government in a top-secret capacity. I can't tell you more than that at the moment. What I can tell you is that we're interested in you working for us when you get out of here."

"Why would you want someone who's been shot in the head and can't even remember his name?"

"We've had our eye on you for a while. As long as the doctors think you're gonna make a full recovery, there's no reason for you not to work for us. As far as your memory, in our line of work, sometimes it's better that way."

"What kind of work is that?"

"Let's get you healthy before we discuss that."

The specialist came into the room and Lawson disappeared from sight. The specialist was a doctor who worked for the organization that flew in with Sanders and Lawson, so they trusted that Nelson could be left alone with him.

Lawson caught up to Sanders outside the hospital as he was finishing up his phone call.

"What's the word?" Lawson asked.

"As soon as he's ready to be moved... he's ours," he responded proudly. "The death certificate is being prepared as we speak. So, you need to get to work right away on preparing the necessary documents and making the notifications."

"I'll get on it."

"I want everything ready to go by the time he's able to leave here."

"What if he's not interested in joining?" she asked.

"What other options does a soldier with a particular set of skills and no memory have? He'll play ball."

After a couple hours of testing, the specialist emerged from Nelson's room.

"What's the word, Doc?" Sanders asked.

"Well, it's one of the most unusual cases I've ever seen."

"In what way?"

"He seems to be fine in every aspect. Now, I've heard of cases where people shot in the head resume their normal lives immediately, so it's not unprecedented, but it is rare."

"So, there's no aftereffects?"

"Well, I didn't say that," the doctor continued. "I asked about his past and he couldn't tell me a thing about it. As far as his motor skills, vision, speech, everything like that seems to check out OK."

"Did you administer the Epideptriol?"

"I did."

"Give you any problems?"

"Nope. Not a bit. Told him it would help stimulate the tissues in his brain and maybe jog his memory."

"Great. Thanks, Doc."

"What's the Epideptriol?" Lawson asked.

"It's an experimental drug. It's designed to attack the part of the brain that controls your memory and kill the tissue," Sanders explained.

"He'll never regain his memory, will he?"

"Not if we can help it. It's in his best interest that he doesn't."

"Why? Why wouldn't you want him to get his memory back?"

"Without going into too many details, there are things in his past that would be better for him if he doesn't remember."

"I see."

"So, you must not ever tell him, even if he asks. That's a direct order," Sanders said.

"How often will the drug be administered?"

"Once a week to start with when possible. Hopefully down the road we won't need it as much, if at all."

Sanders noticed a solemn expression on Lawson's face.

"Don't go getting soft on me now," Sanders said.

"It just seems a shame for a person to go through life without remembering a thing about your past, who you are."

"Maybe it is. But it's what helps keep us in business," Sanders continued. "Let's get back in there and see what he has to say."

It was hard for the government officials to not see the dejection on Nelson's face as they approached his bed. They pulled up a couple of chairs and sat by his side. Nelson was fiddling with his fingernails, trying hard not to look at his visitors. It was embarrassing to not remember a thing about who he was. Sanders and Lawson quietly waited for the fallen soldier to acknowledge their presence. They could see how tough it was for him and didn't want to press him needlessly. A grimace rolled over Nelson's face as he stared down at the covers on his bed. He finally looked up at the pair sitting next to him, water filling up his eyes as he struggled to contain his emotions.

"I've been trying to remember anything... a name, a

face, just something that might trigger the rest of my memory," Nelson began, wiping his eyes. "But I just can't."

"Sometimes it takes time for a person's memory to come back to them," Lawson explained. "Even the simplest thing could bring it back. It could happen right out of the blue."

"She's right," Sanders jumped in. "The key thing to remember is you don't have to fight this battle alone. We're here to help you. We can help get your life back together."

"Why? What's in it for you?" Nelson asked.

"The chance to add an experienced soldier to our staff. There's no question in our minds that your fighting skills could be a great weapon in our arsenal. We think you'd be a valuable piece of our organization," Sanders said.

"What part of the government are you with?"

"Well, that's something we really can't divulge to anyone who's not actively involved with us."

"What if I say no?"

"You're within your right to do so, though we don't see any valid reason why you would want to."

"Maybe I just wanna go home and be with my family."

"Home? Where is that? Can you tell us?" Sanders asked with a sarcastic edge.

Nelson looked away from the pair, angry that he couldn't answer the question.

"I'm sure my family could help get me through it," Nelson said.

"I'm sure they could if you had any," Sanders replied.

"What?"

"Your family could help you if you had any," Sanders repeated, looking at Lawson. "Unfortunately, you don't have any."

"I don't have any family?" Nelson responded dejectedly.

"See for yourself," Sanders said, handing Nelson his file. "From Seattle, Washington, you were the only child born to your parents who died in a car accident two weeks after you graduated high school. It was their deaths that led you to join the military. Alone and nowhere else to go, ten years ago you enlisted."

"No aunts or uncles?"

"One aunt who died from cancer when you were a child, and one uncle, who became a drunk and a petty thief who moved out to California never to be heard from again."

Nelson eagerly read the file, his eyes not moving fast enough for his brain to process the information contained in it. He reread the same passages over and over again, hoping some of it would change by the next time he read it. Sanders and Lawson gave Nelson all the time he needed to read and digest the file, watching his facial expressions as he ate it up. They knew it was something he needed to see to be able to move on from his situation. After half an hour of trying to unfold everything in his mind he finally put the folder down. He looked as confused and aggravated as before.

"Nothing seems familiar," Nelson stated. "Everything is as blank as it was."

"It's something to start with," Lawson replied.

The Cain Conspiracy

"About our job offer," Sanders said. "What do you say?"

"You haven't told me anything about it yet. For all I know I'd be tending sheep."

"Not likely. Slaughtering them maybe."

"I'm not agreeing to anything until you tell me specifics," Nelson said. "You say everything's top secret? I understand that means you avoid saying too much. But unless you get specific I'm not doing anything."

Sanders looked at Lawson, wondering how much he should tell. She nodded as if to spur him on. Within a minute, he started to explain the details of the job offer.

"Without giving away our cover, we work for an ultra-secret agency that targets people who are a threat to the United States," Sanders said.

"You mean terrorists."

"Not necessarily. Could be terrorists, world leaders, dictators, people in a position of power, rebels, perpetrators of major crime, criminal organizations, or anyone that poses a threat or could do so in the near future. It casts a wide net. We're not pigeonholed into any one area. If we believe you're a threat to the United States, either financially, politically, or physically, then we're coming after you."

"And you neutralize the threat?" Nelson asked.

"We eliminate the threat," Sanders succinctly replied.

"You're a kill squad?"

"That's a very narrow way of looking at it, Mr. Nelson. We're not just a kill squad as you put it. Much like the CIA, we assemble mountains of information that may prove valuable to protecting our country."

"You're basically a black ops organization?"

"If that helps you to understand it in its most basic form... yes."

Sanders could see Nelson was thinking about the offer but didn't appear to be fully convinced yet.

"We do not pay people to kill. I can get anybody to do that. I can train a monkey to do that if I wanted to. Any target that's eliminated must be done in a way that completely exonerates the United States. The government does not officially condone or approve of these actions and cannot be implicated in any manner. If it's discovered we're behind some of these missions, it'd be one of the worst scandals in this country's history. Even bigger than Watergate."

"Watergate? What's that?" Nelson asked.

"Google it sometime. To get back on point, you don't get paid to kill. You get paid to be invisible. You get paid to scope out a target, infiltrate that target's territory, eliminate said target, do it without your presence being noticed or compromised, and without any involvement suspected of the United States. To take it even further, your life as it stands right now will be gone. You cannot be arrested, put in jail, appear in traffic court, criminal court, divorce court, or any court. Your picture cannot appear in any newspaper. Your name won't return any information in a computer, and your fingerprint won't come up in any database. To put it bluntly, you... do not exist."

"Why are you hung up on getting me? I'm sure you could get a thousand other guys to do the same work."

"You're a highly trained soldier, part of Team Delta. In addition, you've sustained an injury that we can easily pass off into your implied death. You also have nobody back home who would miss you or poke around into your disappearance," Sanders continued.

"My implied death?"

"As I said, once you begin working for us, you do not exist. You're officially dead. That means after you leave this room Thomas Nelson ceases to exist. He died on the operating table."

"How much time do I have to think about it?" Nelson asked.

"Oh, about ten minutes," Sanders replied, looking down at his watch.

Nelson looked up at the man standing next to his bed, wondering how he could expect him to make a life altering decision so quickly. He sat in silence, his face showing no expression, staring at Sanders. A numb feeling overtook his body. He slowly shifted his gaze over to Lawson, his face still void of life, taking it all in. He sat there digesting the information he'd just been given. Was it the life he wanted? To be a soulless, ruthless killer who had no past and didn't even exist? He thought about how changing his name would affect him, but considering he couldn't remember anything anyway, it really was of no consequence what anyone called him. After a few minutes of thought he shook his head in acknowledgment, reluctantly accepting the offer, knowing he didn't have many other options. At least with them he'd be a part of something. A group he could rely on and help him fill in any missing pieces, or questions he'd have. If he declined and went on his own, he had no family, and no one to turn to. That was an even scarier proposition for someone who couldn't remember anything.

"Well, I can't even express how happy I am right now," Sanders said. "Welcome to the team."

"Thanks."

"Sorry about changing the name but it has to be done."

"It's OK. I can't remember anything so it's not doing me much good anyway," Nelson stated.

"I can understand."

"So, what's my new name?"

"Matthew Cain."

3

Two weeks later—Sanders and his entourage of officials boarded the jet, bound for New York. Cain slipped into a seat against the window, staring at the landscape below as the ground became a blip on the radar.

"So, how'd you come up with Matthew Cain?" Cain asked.

"We give new agents new identities once they start working with us. We name them after people in the biggest organization ever created," Sanders replied.

"What's that?"

"The Bible."

"So, who do you name them after?"

"Killers. Seemed more fitting."

"Who am I named after?"

"Cain. He murdered his brother Abel and was the world's first murderer," Sanders said.

"That's comforting. So where am I gonna live when we get there?" Cain asked.

"Everything's been taken care of," Sanders replied. "You've got a nice apartment in the heart of New York City."

"Once we get back, you'll be given a package of everything you'll need," Lawson interjected. "Bank account, credit cards, car, passports, driver's license, everything."

"You'll notice that $250,000 has been deposited into your bank account to start with. Once we see that you're going to stay with us for a while you will get $500,000 deposited into your account every six months, the first of January and July."

"Nice."

"Money will be the least of your worries. Make no mistake, though, you will earn every penny of it," Sanders added.

"What if I don't like living in New York?"

"You only have to stay there for a brief period. We want to make sure you're completely comfortable with the operation. After that, you're free to live wherever you like. More times than not you'll be off on an assignment, anyway. One of the trade-offs of that money is that you will be on call 24/7. You will make yourself available at any time of the day no matter where you are. If you are needed on an assignment immediately, you are to drop what you're doing and respond at a moment's notice," Lawson explained. "It is rare when that happens as we like to plan missions out a few days in advance, but it does happen and you will be available."

"That's not a problem. I obviously have nothing or no one to tie me down."

"That's the other thing I wanted to talk to you about. At one point this agency frowned upon agents having exterior relationships as they felt it would interfere in plans and at some point cause friction. What we found was some agents began to snap. Loneliness set in, there was nobody waiting for them, nothing to keep them going, and the stress of the missions wore them down. Now the policy is that we encourage you to make friendships and relationships outside of this agency. We want you to be happy and content and in return hopefully agents won't go off the deep end. The conditions are that you cannot tell them what you do. If you want to tell them you work in insurance, or sales, or even for the government, that is up to you. But your work here is top secret."

"And I'll even take it a step further," Sanders chimed in. "You're paid handsomely for your work here and in return for that we expect to be your number one priority. I don't really care what you do or say when you're at home as long as this agency is not involved. We are an ultra top-secret department and we must remain that way. Any slips by you about our work here to a friend, girlfriend, wife, reporter, anybody, will result in their immediate death... and probably yours. There are no reprieves and it's non-conditional. Is that clear?"

"I understand. How long will I be needed to do this?" Cain asked.

"There's no set timetable. We ask for ten or fifteen years. Anything after that will be evaluated on a case-by-case basis," Lawson said. "If you choose to walk away at that point you'll have fifteen million dollars in your bank account and free to live the rest of your life however you choose, though you'll forever be bound by the rules of disclosure about this agency."

"What about guns?"

"You'll be given your choice of weapons at the Center. Though you won't always travel with them. Due to airport security and customs, sometimes you'll need to acquire your weapon once you arrive at your target location. Typically, it's not a problem as we have operators and safety deposit boxes all over the world. Obtaining a weapon will be the least of your problems."

"What Center?"

"It's where our headquarters are."

"It'd probably be best to get some sleep if you can," Sanders said. "You'll need it once we get back."

Cain took Sanders up on the suggestion and dozed off for a while. They arrived in New York late that night, company cars waiting for them once they touched down. Sanders, Lawson, and Cain were driven away in the lead car with the other officers in the trailing car. Cain stared out the window intently, looking at the scenery.

"Have I ever been here before?" Cain asked. He could see the confusion in the faces of his companions once the words left his lips. "In New York, I mean."

"Not to my knowledge," Sanders replied.

A short time later they arrived at the Center, going into the underground parking garage. As they got out of the car, Cain took note of his surroundings. It was a natural instinct for him, something that he still remembered from his military days. He always had to be aware of what was around him, noting any possible trouble spots, no matter how peaceful or innocent something looked. This was one of those times when something just didn't feel right. He looked at the faces of Sanders and Lawson, who didn't seem troubled by anything, but still felt like something was off. They went inside the elevator, where Sanders pushed the button to go up to the lobby. Once the doors opened and they stepped off the elevator, they were surprised to find three armed men waiting for them, guns pointed at each of their faces.

"Anyone moves and you're all dead," one of the men yelled.

All three of the intruding men were wearing black masks and two were armed with AK-47s while the other just had a pistol. They forced Sanders, Lawson, and Cain onto the ground, lying on their stomachs.

"What do you want with us? Money?" Sanders asked.

"We don't want money. We want him," one of the men replied, pointing at Cain.

"He's new to our company. He doesn't know anything."

"We'll see about that."

One of the men pulled out another black mask, though this one didn't have any holes for the mouth or eyes. They sat Cain up and put the hood over his head. They stood him up as one of the men took the butt end of his rifle and smashed it into Cain's face. Cain immediately dropped to the floor as the blunt force temporarily knocked him out. Two of the assailants each grabbed one of Cain's arms and dragged him back into the elevator. The leader of the group kept Sanders and Lawson on the ground at gunpoint before joining the other two in the elevator.

About an hour later Cain started coming out of it. He emitted a low moan while moving his head. He opened his eyes but only saw darkness with the hood still over his head. A few seconds later the hood was pulled off. He tried to move his arms, but they were restrained, tied behind his back as he sat on an old wooden chair. Cain squinted, trying to adjust to the bright lights. He looked around the room but he was alone. There was nothing else even in the room other than the chair he was sitting on. There was a small mirror on the opposite side of the room. After sitting there for five minutes, wondering what his abductors had planned for him, someone finally entered the room. He was a middle-aged man, graying hair around his temples, and dressed in an expensive suit. He circled Cain a couple of times before speaking up.

"I'll start this out by explaining a few things to you," the man said. "I'm gonna get the information I want out of you one way or another. I'd prefer to do it the easy way. I'll ask you a question and you simply answer it honestly. If you'd rather do it the hard way, then I'm not opposed to that either. In that instance, we'll simply beat the information out of you using whatever kinds of torture amuses us at the moment. Understand?"

"Sure," Cain replied.

"First off, let's start with your name."

"Peter."

"Peter what?"

"Peter Pan," Cain said seriously.

"Peter Pan," his interrogator repeated with a laugh. "Somehow I don't think so."

"OK. My name really is Peter."

"Peter what?"

"Peter Rabbit."

The well-dressed man wasn't as amused with this answer as he was the one before it. He motioned toward the mirror for someone to come in. Seconds later two more men entered the room. Both were younger men, in their mid-twenties probably, and as well dressed as their superior.

"See if you can make him a little more willing," the elder man told them.

Cain knew what that meant and his face tensed up as he tried to prepare for what was about to happen. He closed his eyes just as a clenched right fist made contact with his jaw, knocking him and his chair on the ground. The other man pulled him up in time for a left hand to put him back onto the ground, the man's knuckles hitting Cain across the bridge of his nose. One of the men pulled him back up and immediately took the wind out of Cain by punching him in the stomach several times.

"I'll ask you one more time. Your name?" the leader asked.

Cain took a deep breath before answering. "It's Michael."

"Michael what?"

"Michael Jordan."

"You're a funny man," he said after letting out a laugh. He seemed rather amused by Cain's sense of humor.

"Not as funny as your face is gonna look after I'm done rearranging it," Cain threatened.

"Well, we'll see about that. Take Mr. Cain away for a bit and see how he likes the dark."

Cain looked at the man before him curiously, wondering how he knew his name and why he was trying to beat it out of him if he already knew it.

"Yes, Mr. Cain, I'm already aware of who you are," he said.

"Then why the muscle?"

"I told you I was prepared to do things either way you chose. I wanted to see which way you preferred. Apparently, you like to make things hard on yourself. So, we'll do it your way."

The younger men untied Cain, lifting him up from the chair. As they began walking, Cain tripped one of them then punched the other one, catching him off guard. Cain kicked both men as they lay on the ground. Once they were incapacitated he turned his attention to the leader who was just standing against the wall watching the activities. Cain put his hands around his neck but was soon met with resistance as several more men rushed into the room to stop him. They pulled Cain off the man and restrained him.

"What do you want with me?" Cain yelled.

"In due time, Mr. Cain. In due time," the leader replied.

The men put the hood back over Cain's head and led him out of the room. They walked him down a long, cold hallway that had bare white walls with a few doors on each side. They bypassed these doors until they reached the end of the hallway, a single door remaining. Once they reached their destination, they opened the door and shoved Cain in, quickly closing the door behind him. Cain's hands weren't tied together, so he pulled the hood off. The room was pitch black. Cain used his hands to feel around the edge of the room. He walked around the entire room, not feeling anything that would indicate a window or opening of any kind. He felt the door but there didn't seem to be a handle on it so he assumed it could only be opened from the outside.

The captors could see into the room through a piece

of glass along part of the wall. Once they saw Cain sit down on the floor, they left to convene in the meeting room. They went into the room, where the man who ordered it all was already waiting for them.

"What did you think?" the well-dressed leader asked his superior.

"Nicely done," Director Sanders responded, smiling.

"Sir, do you really think this is necessary?" Shelly Lawson asked, concerned about Cain's condition.

"Unless you can think of another way in which case I'm all ears. We don't have time to subject him to six to eight months of intensive training to see what he can do. The best way to see him in action and see how he responds to situations is to throw him into a situation where he thinks his life is at risk."

"I just hope we don't lose him after this."

"We won't."

"How long should we keep him in solitary?" the well-dressed man asked.

"Leave him there for a week. We'll see how that changes him," Sanders replied. "Any objections, Shelly?"

"No," Lawson replied after a long pause.

Sanders ordered Cain to be kept locked up for a week, with no outside contact, except for one meal a day. He wanted to see how he'd act after being in a weakened state from not eating and being in constant darkness. Sanders stopped by to check on him every day to see if his demeanor started changing. Though it was tough on Cain not knowing what time of day it was or what was happening to him, he tried to use the time to his advantage. Though they were trying to starve him and make him weak, he tried to combat it and stay strong by doing pushups and sit-ups. He slept a lot and tried to not let his mind wander and think positively. He figured that they wanted him alive for some reason or they would've killed him already.

After a week had passed the same two men who worked him over before came in to get him.

"Smells like piss in here," one of them stated.

"I wanted it to smell like you were at home," Cain remarked, earning him a kick in the stomach.

"C'mon, it's time for another chat."

They dragged Cain up to his feet, helping him stand. He was a little weak but was able to stand on his own and walk by himself. There was another guard standing outside the room as they walked into the hallway and led him down the hallway into another room. It was the same room they interrogated him in before. This time he wasn't tied to a chair. All three men guarded the room before the well-dressed leader walked in.

"Looks like solitary confinement wasn't too harsh for you."

"Was a little too bright for my liking," Cain said sarcastically.

"Your humor serves you well."

"What do you want?"

"Who do you work for?"

"I don't know."

"Why are you in New York?"

"I don't know."

"Why were you with Sanders?"

"I don't know who that is."

"C'mon now, you don't know who you were with or where you are? You expect me to believe that?"

"I don't care what you believe."

"You should. Because the only way you're getting out of here is if you start making me believe what you're saying."

"Look, I've got a bullet in my head and I have memory issues. Doctors say I have something called sporadic amnesia. Sometimes I can't remember what happened an hour ago. As far as this Sanders guy, maybe I know him, but I just can't remember right now."

"Maybe you just need your memory jogged a little."

The leader motioned to one of the guards who stepped in front of Cain and belted him with a right hand, knocking Cain to the ground. As they helped Cain back to his chair, he noticed a gun inside the left jacket of one of the guards.

"The next time someone hits me it'll be the last mistake they make," Cain said, hoping it'd provoke them into doing it again.

It worked as the same man stepped in front of him. He rose his arm up, ready to pounce, when Cain sprung up from the chair. He reached inside the man's jacket and pulled out his gun, quickly firing into his midsection. He fell to the ground and Cain turned around and fired at the other two guards, hitting them in the chest before they had a chance to remove their weapons. Cain then turned his sights on the leader of the group who looked shocked at what just happened. He wasn't armed and started backpedaling toward the wall. Cain circled around him as the man kept walking backwards until he found himself in the middle of the room. Cain made him sit in the chair as he started his own line of questions.

"Where am I?" Cain asked.

"New York."

"Who are you?"

"The Easter Bunny."

Cain wasn't amused and backhanded the man with the butt of the gun, smacking him across the side of his face.

"Who put you up to this?"

"Santa Claus."

Cain smacked him again with the gun, knocking him to the ground, and causing a deep cut on the man's forehead.

"Last chance to tell me what you know," Cain said.

The man stayed silent and Cain thought about putting a bullet in him but ultimately decided against it and instead kicked him across the face as he broke for the exit. Cain peeked out the door and didn't see anyone else out there and started down the hallway when lights and sirens started going off. He raced down the hallway and tried to open any doors he came across but they were all locked. Suddenly, he heard a commotion behind him as he turned around and saw a few men running toward him. He fired a couple shots in their direction and kept moving. He came across another door that was also locked but tried kicking it open. He knew he had to get the door open somehow or else he'd get captured again. He wasn't going to be able to fend them off forever in that hallway. Cain desperately tried to open the door without any success. As the men moved closer, he fired a few more shots. He ran out of bullets when the door suddenly opened behind him. He turned around and was shocked to see Sanders standing there. Since he wasn't restrained in any way, Cain assumed Sanders was somehow involved in his kidnapping.

"Hello, Cain," Sanders said.

"What the hell are you doing to me?" Cain yelled.

Cain put his hands on the collar of Sanders' suit, ready to shake some answers out of him. Instead, Cain got knocked out cold, hit from behind as one of the guards slammed a gun into the back of his head.

"Take him to my office," Sanders told them.

"What do you think?" the lead training officer asked.

"I think he'll do nicely," Sanders replied.

"I'm not sure it's the best test for him."

"He's a former member of Delta Force. We already know he's received great training. He doesn't need more of that. I think we saw exactly what we needed to see."

"Which was?"

"He's willing and able to kill at a moment's notice, without hesitation. He'll do what it takes to survive. Those are the most important characteristics that an agent needs. Everything else is gravy. Those are the attributes that some men don't possess. He does. He has them and he'll use them."

They took Cain to Sanders' office, laying him on a couch, where he lay motionless for a couple of hours. Once he started coming out of it he looked up at the ceiling for a few seconds. He quickly remembered what transpired and jumped off the couch ready for a fight with someone. He scanned the room and after seeing no one, stood at ease. Cain looked at the pictures on the walls and walked over to the desk. He began rummaging through the drawers, not sure what he was looking for, but hoping to find anything that might explain what was going on. He took some papers out of the bottom drawer and saw a revolver sitting there. He heard the handle of the door jiggle and grabbed the gun. He pointed it toward the door and was ready to fire as soon as it opened. Cain was surprised to see Sanders and Lawson walk through the door. The pair stopped in their tracks once they saw the gun pointed at them.

"Put that thing away," Sanders said.

"Give me one good reason why I shouldn't blow your head off right now," Cain replied. "You set me up."

"The first good reason is that you can't. There's no bullets in that gun."

Cain briefly looked at the gun while it was still pointed at Sanders and pulled the trigger.

"Lucky for me I wasn't bluffing," Sanders noted.

Cain sighed and felt defeated already as he tossed the gun on the desk.

"Sit down so we can talk," Sanders said.

Cain ignored his wishes and continued to stand in a somewhat adversarial manner.

"Please," Sanders said, trying to de-escalate the situation. "Sit down."

Cain looked at Lawson who nodded in agreement. After a few seconds of deliberating, he decided to comply, realizing he didn't really have any other options but to comply with their wishes. He sat back down on the couch as Sanders sat on the edge of his desk.

"Everything you just went through was a test," Sanders said calmly.

"A test?" Cain snapped.

"Typically, a new agent requires intensive field training that lasts anywhere from six months to a year.

With your military background, I thought waiting might not be in our best interest. I wanted to get you out in the field as soon as possible but I needed to see how good you were to bypass the training. So, we devised this plan so nobody would get hurt but we'd find out about your abilities."

"I shot three men for a test."

"Wax bullets. I made sure all weapons were fitted with them for safety purposes. The men you shot are all fine."

"You intentionally left me in a dark room, trying to starve me to death."

"We had to see if you'd start to break. And we weren't trying to starve you, we gave you a sandwich every day."

"On stale bread."

"I'll have a word with our chef."

"So, how'd I do?"

"You did exceptional. I have no concerns. If we put you out in the field tomorrow, I'd expect outstanding results. If anything doesn't go according to plan, I can see you have the necessary attributes to..." Sanders explained before his voice trailed off.

"To what?" Cain asked.

"To survive."

Cain sat there digesting the information, not sure what he should be feeling. Sanders could see Cain still had some doubts.

"Look, I can understand you're a little agitated right now and I don't blame you for it at all," Sanders began. "But this is a tough business we're in. It's not for the weak minded or weak-hearted. We need to make sure who we're sending out there is up to the task. If you wanna go home and be pissed off for a while that's OK. But we think you'll be an asset to this agency and we think we can be an asset to you if you want help in trying to get your memory back."

As Cain pondered Sanders words his initial anger slowly started to subside. He still wasn't sure what they did was necessary to see what he could do, but he knew he would need some help in regaining his memory. He didn't know who else he would be able to turn to.

"I tell you what, why don't you go home and just think about things for a while. If you decide this isn't right for you, we won't stand in your way. You're free to go," Sanders told him. "But I think you'll come to the proper decision that this is where you belong. The right decision."

"Go home? Where's that?" Cain asked.

"We set you up with an apartment a few blocks from here. I'll have someone take you there. Relax for a little bit."

Cain knew he didn't need to relax for a while, or think about it for a few hours. He was in. He figured if anyone had the resources to help him get his memory back it'd be the government. He'd overlook this little stunt they created and do what was asked of him as long as the tricks ended there.

"I don't need time to think," Cain said, standing up. "I'll do it. But if anyone pulls something like this on me again, I will make them wish they hadn't."

"Understood," Sanders responded, smirking.

"I'll take you to your place," Lawson said.

"Before you leave, as a show of good faith, go over to

the gun room," Sanders said. "Pick out something you like."

As Cain and Lawson left the room, Sanders pulled out his cell phone to make a call.

"Hey, it's me," Sanders said. "Are you free right now?"

"Yeah," the voice on the other line replied.

"Good. I have a job for you right now. He's on his way to his place in a few minutes. Could you be there waiting for him as a surprise?"

"Sure."

"Good. I'll pay you the usual fee."

Lawson led Cain to the gun room, where it looked like they had several hundred guns lined up. It was a small room that had a few tables locked together, not to mention shelves on the wall that were fully stocked with guns and ammunition. If the building was ever stormed by enemies they certainly had enough weapons and ammo to make the fight last a while. There were cameras at the door and inside the room to make sure nobody was taking guns out that was unauthorized. Cain walked around the room, carefully analyzing some of the pieces, picking a few up to get a feel for them. A couple felt really comfortable to him, perhaps because they were active military weapons, which he probably had used previously even if he didn't remember it. His eyes caught sight of a Sig Sauer M11 on the table. He picked it up and pointed it at the wall, instantly knowing he wanted it. He put it inside the back of his belt as he picked up a Glock 19, analyzing it thoroughly. He also shoved that inside his belt as he grabbed some ammunition boxes off the shelf.

"I'm taking these two," Cain stated.

"Planning on starting your own little war?" Lawson replied.

"I like to be prepared."

"That's fine."

Once they left, they went down to the garage, finding Lawson's car. As they drove away, Lawson wanted to get to know her new agent better.

"I just want to let you know I wasn't in favor of what they did to you this past week," she said.

"You weren't?"

"No. I didn't think it was necessary, but I was overruled."

"It's fine. Thanks for the concern though," Cain said. "So how long have you been working here?"

"Seven years."

"You like it?"

"For the most part. Like any other job, you have good days and bad. Some days are more stressful than others. But yeah, I do."

"How'd you get mixed up in this?"

"I worked for the FBI as an analyst. One day, out of the blue, I was approached about a new agency that was starting. It was top secret, completely off the books, that nobody knew about. It seemed exciting, so I joined up," Lawson said.

"I don't even know what it's called."

"We have no official name. Unofficially we're known as The Specter Project, or Project Specter."

"Is there a meaning behind that?"

"Specter means ghost, or a source of terror."

"I guess that does fit, huh? So, you're telling me

nobody knows this agency exists? How's that possible?" Cain asked.

"I don't have all the answers either. I only know what they want me to know. He wasn't lying when he said this is an ultra-secret agency. As far as I can tell Sanders only reports to three or four people. Who those people are I don't know."

"I thought the CIA did this type of stuff."

"The CIA has become too well known to do many of the tasks we're now doing. Plus, there's too much red tape. Due to political pressures, they'd simply be unable to do some of the things we do. We're a completely unknown Black Ops division."

They continued talking about the organization for a few minutes until they wound up at Cain's apartment building.

"Well, here we are," Lawson said, handing Cain the keys to his apartment. "Eighth floor."

"Thanks. What happens tomorrow?"

"Nothing. Now you wait for us to contact you about an assignment. Just take it easy."

4

Cain went into the building and took the elevator up to his apartment. He stood in front of the door, trying to shake the feeling that something wasn't right, and stared at the door for a few moments. He unlocked it, and pushed it open without stepping inside. He took a few steps in, carefully surveying his surroundings, trying to notice if anything seemed strange. Suddenly, music started blaring from the bedroom, the door flying open. Cain immediately withdrew the Glock pistol from his belt, waiting for a figure to emerge in the doorway. A few seconds later the outline of his visitor became visible, causing Cain to relax the finger he had pressed on the trigger. He let his arm fall to the side, the pistol bouncing off his leg. The scantily clad woman dancing in his bedroom eased any fears he previously had. Cain put the pistol back in his belt before barging past the tight skirted blonde, whose ample cleavage was barely contained in her dress. He didn't pay much mind to her as he found the booming stereo and turned it off.

"Wrong kind of music?" she innocently asked.

Cain walked past her, once again not looking at her, on his way to the kitchen. He grabbed a bottle of water from the refrigerator and sat down on a bar stool at the counter, finally looking at his visitor.

"Who are you? What do you want? And how'd you get in here?" Cain finally asked.

"I have a special key," she teased. "And I'm your birthday present."

"It's not my birthday."

"Well, then I guess it's just your lucky day."

Cain continued to just sit there drinking his water. The woman was starting to get confused, unsure of Cain's uninterested behavior. She hadn't encountered that kind of resistance before.

"So, if you don't want me to dance what would you like me to do?" she asked. "Should I wait in bed for you?"

"Actually, I'd kind of like you to leave," Cain replied.

"What?"

"I don't know who put you up to this but I'm not interested."

"You're not interested? How can you not be interested? What's wrong with you? Are you some kind of weirdo or something?"

"I guess you could say that," Cain said as he got up to open the door.

The woman sighed and walked over to him. She closed the door and slowly caressed his chest with her fingers. Cain closed his eyes and grabbed her wrists, moving them off his body. He went back over to the counter to grab his water. The woman followed him.

"Is there something wrong with me? Not your type? What?"

"You're a beautiful woman. But I'm just not interested right now," Cain said.

"Wow. You're really a challenge, aren't you?"

Cain rolled his eyes, unsure of what else he could say to get the woman to leave, and walked over to the couch.

"Look, I'm tired, I've had a long day, and I really just want to relax for a little bit," Cain said.

"That's what I'm here for. To help you relax. Listen, if we don't do anything here then I don't get paid," she said in frustration.

"Who's paying you?"

"Sanders."

"Why?"

"He uses me every now and then for his employees."

"Do you know what we do?" Cain asked.

"I just know that you work for the government. Sanders says you guys are in frequent high-stress situations and need to get the tension out."

Cain grinned and let out a slight laugh.

"So, does that mean you're ready?" the woman asked hopefully.

"What's your name, anyway?"

"Destiny."

Cain looked at her, tilted his head and raised his eyebrows in amusement.

"Destiny? Really? What's your real name?" Cain asked.

"That is my real name."

"You gotta do better than that."

The woman looked up, biting her lip, and reluctantly replied. "Heather. Listen, I'd really like to get paid for this, so if you're still not interested, just sit back and I'll do all the work."

"You're persistent."

"I get paid a lot of money for this."

"How's Sanders gonna know nothing happened if you just walked out of here right now?" Cain asked.

"I don't know, it's Sanders, he knows everything. Wouldn't surprise me if he had this place bugged or cameras somewhere."

"Well, if it makes you feel better, you can stay awhile," Cain said as he lay on the couch.

"That's more like it," she replied as she walked toward him.

"Oh, no, no, you can sit on that one," he said, pointing to the sofa across from them.

"I can't believe this," she whispered to herself as she walked to the sofa, sitting down.

"If it helps, if anyone asks, I'll tell them you were great," Cain said.

"Thanks. Are we gonna do anything at all tonight?"

"Yeah. We can talk if you want."

"Talk? That's it? Just talk?"

"Well, I guess if you're hungry you can help yourself to the fridge."

"Are you always this difficult?"

"Mostly."

Cain grabbed the remote off the coffee table and turned the TV on. He flipped channels until he came across a documentary on black ops on The History Channel. He intently watched the program for the next half hour as Heather tended to her nails in boredom. Once the show ended Cain sat up and looked at Heather.

"Oh, is it over now?" she asked sarcastically.

"Oh, you still here?" he replied as he took a sip of water. "So why do you do this?"

"Why not? I like to have sex and I get paid a lot of money."

"Seems like you could be doing something more..."

"Dignified, maybe? More important? Like solving the world's hunger problem or finding a cure for cancer or something?"

"Maybe. You're an attractive girl. I'm sure there's a lot of other opportunities out there for you."

"Oh, there is. I also work at a strip club."

"You seem pretty proud of it."

"Hey, it pays the bills."

"So, what're you gonna do when the looks fade, and the dance moves are gone?" Cain asked.

"By that time, hopefully I'll have enough money saved where I won't have to worry about it."

"Is that what you're doing with all your money, saving it?"

"Is it really any of your business?" she asked.

"You're in my apartment, sitting on my couch, and watching my TV. If you don't like the questions, you can leave anytime you want."

"Fine. My goal is to save up a couple hundred thousand and then leave this city. Move to the country somewhere, buy a nice little house, and start my own business," she revealed.

"That's a lot of money."

"It is. I've still got a few years to go."

"What kind of business?"

"I don't know. Maybe something that involves the marketing degree I have."

"How does a girl with a marketing degree wind up here?"

"A lot of debt."

"Your parents approve of what you're doing?" Cain asked.

"My mother died when I was five. My father, if you can call him that, raised me until I was about seventeen. Then I left on my own."

"Didn't get along?"

"I was tired of the verbal assaults and physical beatings," Heather said.

"Sorry to hear that."

"Yeah. Met a guy who wanted me to get into that kind of life, and like a sucker I wanted to please him. Then a few months later he ran off with another dancer. There I was, stuck."

"Still could've left," Cain said.

"Guess I didn't know what else to do. Should've went with my sister."

"You have a sister?"

"Four years younger than me. She went to school to become a teacher. Haven't talked to her in a few years. She disapproved of my lifestyle," she said.

"Where's she at now?"

"I don't even know."

Cain sat there looking at Heather, nodding, with an approving look on his face. He liked that there seemed to be some substance to her, and that she wasn't just a pretty face with no ambition.

"How about a drink?" Cain offered.

"Sure."

Heather watched Cain head to the kitchen, actually admiring him now that he didn't just jump all over her the moment he laid eyes on her. She put up the front with most men she came in contact with and pretended to love everything about what she did. She found most men offered extra tips when they thought she was really into them and all about the sex.

"Sorry, don't have anything stronger," Cain said with a wide grin, handing her a bottle of water.

Heather smiled. "That'll be fine."

Cain walked back around the coffee table, sitting on the couch across from Heather. He sat up at attention, eager to learn more about his companion.

"So, what about you? How'd you end up working for Sanders?"

"I was in the military. I was on the verge of leaving and he offered me a job," Cain said.

"You like it?"

"Well, I just started."

Cain sat back and stared at the ceiling, suddenly not feeling well. He wiped sweat off his forehead with his arm.

"Are you OK? You don't look so good," Heather said.

Cain put his right hand up to his ear, hearing a loud ringing sound. He squinted as he couldn't see with the bright lights shining in his eyes. A few seconds later his eyes closed entirely to block out the color streaks. Heather rushed over to the phone and called Sanders, as she was instructed to do in case there was an emergency with any of his guys. Sanders informed her when he first hired her that if things ever got out of hand in any manner that he was the first one to be called, and he would handle it, with no police or medical personnel involved.

"Hey, something's wrong with your guy here," she screamed.

"What's wrong?"

"I don't know. He's not looking good," she said, glancing over at him.

"I'll have someone there in ten minutes."

"Oh my God," she yelled as she watched him fall on his side.

"What now?"

"I think he just passed out."

Sanders hung up and had a doctor rush over to Cain's apartment. Heather ran over to Cain, who was now lying on his side on the couch. She lifted his eyelids open and checked his pulse. She really wasn't sure what she was doing, but it seemed like a good thing to do. She stood up and put her hands on her head, hastily trying to think of what else she could do. Two minutes later, Cain opened his eyes, not totally sure what was going on. He was breathing heavy and batting his eyelids, trying to get his wits about him.

"Are you OK?" Heather asked.

Cain slowly sat up and looked at her, unsure what had happened. Heather grabbed his arm to try to comfort him.

"Do you need anything?" Heather asked again.

A dazed and confused look appeared in Cain's eyes,

still hazy from passing out. He had no idea who the beautiful woman sitting next to him was.

"Who are you?" he asked.

"You don't remember?"

"No," he replied with a shake of his head. "What happened?"

"I don't know. We were just talking and all of a sudden you just looked really bad and then slumped over."

"I passed out?"

"Yes."

"For how long?"

"Maybe two or three minutes. I called Sanders. He's sending a doctor here to check you out."

"Who's Sanders?"

"Umm... your boss," she responded, unsure of what else to say.

"Oh. Who are you again?"

"I'm Heather."

"Do I know you?"

"We just met earlier," she told him.

Cain leaned forward and attempted to get up but was met with resistance from Heather, who gently held him back.

"Just sit back until the doctor gets here," Heather said. "What do you need? I'll get it for you."

"I'm thirsty."

Heather grabbed the bottle of water from the coffee table and helped Cain take a sip of it. She laid him back down on the couch and kneeled down on the floor next to him, watching over him. A few minutes later they heard keys rattling in the door, a second later the door opening to reveal Sanders, Lawson, and the doctor. The trio rushed into the apartment and immediately checked on Cain's condition.

"I said give him a good time, Heather, I didn't say kill him," Sanders remarked.

Heather rolled her eyes, ignoring the comment, and watched as the doctor looked at Cain. Several minutes later the doctor got up and approached Heather, Sanders, and Lawson, who were standing in a circle.

"He had a seizure," the doctor noted as he turned to look at his patient.

"I thought the drugs were supposed to stop that," Sanders said.

"For most patients, the drugs will control them, but it doesn't mean he can't have additional seizures. The drugs also have side effects, including dizziness, nausea, vision problems, and memory issues."

"Is this gonna be a frequent problem?" Sanders asked.

"He might have a few a year or he might never have another one. No one can say with any amount of certainty. Everybody reacts differently."

"Just great. Every time this guy's out in the field we're gonna be wondering if he collapses and falls off a cliff somewhere."

"What do we do from here?" Lawson asked.

"Well, I'd give him a couple of days to rest and recover. No strenuous activity," the doctor replied. "After that he should be able to resume normal activities."

"What about his memory, doctor?" Heather asked.

"What about it?"

"Well, when he woke up, he didn't know who I was or recognize Mr. Sanders' name."

"Oh, well, that's quite normal. Often when someone

has a seizure, their mind is still cloudy and can't recognize names or faces. It usually wears off within thirty minutes or an hour and he should be able to recognize anyone he knew before."

They talked amongst themselves for the next few minutes trying to decide how to proceed. They didn't feel comfortable leaving Cain by himself in case anything else happened.

"I guess I'll stay here with him," Lawson volunteered.

"No, you're too valuable to stay here. You've got work to do and ten other agents to take care of. I can't have you sitting here being a nursemaid," Sanders responded.

"Who do you have in mind then? Who else is aware of his problem and will be able to stay with him?"

Sanders walked over to the window, looked down at the traffic below, and thought about who he could get.

"I could stay with him," Heather blurted out.

Sanders raised his eyebrows, surprised at the stripper's suggestion. He turned around and locked eyes with Lawson, also shocked at Heather's offer. Heather knew that as soon as she said it they would look at her strangely and wonder why she was making the offer. She wasn't quite sure herself, except it just seemed like the right thing to do. Sanders could tell by Lawson's face that she was not in favor of it. He then walked over to Heather to discuss it further with her.

"Why would you wanna do that?" he asked.

"He seems like a nice guy."

"Strange coming from you."

"Sir, I really don't think this is a good idea," Lawson said.

"Why not? Someone's gotta look after him. Who else do you have in mind?"

"We can get someone at the office to swing by. One of the secretaries maybe."

"And who's gonna take their spot? There's a lot of important work to be done. I'm not sure that's the best and most productive use of time."

"What does she know about taking care of someone? Plus, we can't afford to have any information slip out by accident."

"What of your other job?" Sanders asked.

"I'll take a few days off," Heather replied.

"Everything here is top secret information, you understand that? Any slips about his condition to the wrong people could mean his death. Or yours. Nothing leaves this room."

"Who am I gonna tell?" Heather said, incredulous that he suspected her of revealing anything. "I don't even know anything other than you work for the government."

"I'm just making sure we understand each other."

"We do. Nobody will know of his condition."

"I can't reimburse you for your time, other than what you were already here for."

"I'm not asking for anything."

Sanders took a step back and paced back and forth for a few moments, deliberating and considering his options. It didn't take long for him to come to a conclusion.

"Well, I don't think we have very many alternatives to Ms. Lloyd's offer. I think we should be appreciative of her being a good Samaritan. So, considering that, I think it'd be in our best interest to accept her kind offer," Sanders said.

Lawson slightly opened her mouth, ready to continue fighting against the notion, but she thought better of it. She rarely went against Sanders' wishes, and when she did, it was something she really believed in fighting for. She wasn't sure this was a big enough deal to go against him. She sighed in disapproval, looking Heather up and down in her revealing outfit, but didn't fight the directive any further. Although she disagreed with his decision, she understood.

"Well, we have other matters to attend to, so we're gonna get going," Sanders said. "Anything happens, anything you need, you call me."

"I will," Heather said.

As the trio of officials got to the door, Sanders stopped and looked back at Heather.

"Remember what the doctor said, no strenuous activity," Sanders said sarcastically.

"I heard," she shot back.

5

Heather walked back over to the couch and placed her hand on Cain's forehead. She then helped him take another sip of water and sat on the sofa across from him. About a half hour later the fuzziness began wearing off and he finally recognized the woman in his apartment. He started to ask more questions but Heather wanted to make sure he just took it easy the rest of the night. Cain continued to lay there, lethargic for the next couple of hours, as the two of them watched TV. Heather watched him fall asleep as the midnight hour approached. She went into the bedroom, grabbed a blanket off the bed, and placed it over him. She fell asleep on the sofa a short time later.

Cain woke up the next morning much more alert, the cloudiness seemingly gone from his head. He actually felt pretty good as he lay there looking up at the ceiling, waiting for the sleepiness to wear off. Something smelled pretty good, encouraging him to finally get up. He walked over to the kitchen to find Heather making breakfast.

"You can cook too, huh?" Cain asked, smiling.

"I've been known to cook a few things," she said, smiling back. "It's only eggs and bacon. It's kinda hard to mess that up."

"I've known people who could mess up peanut butter and jelly."

Heather let out a good laugh, "I'm sure you have."

"Smells really good," Cain admitted.

"Sit down. It's almost ready."

Cain sat at the table and noticed that Heather seemed to be wearing a man's shirt. Most likely his. He couldn't complain too much since it did look pretty good on her. It only covered a third of her thigh, but he certainly had no qualms about looking at her nicely tanned legs.

"Nice shirt," he blurted out. "Something looks familiar about it."

"Oh. Yeah. Sorry about that." She sheepishly smiled. "I wasn't planning on being here more than a few hours last night so I had no other clothes. Hope you don't mind."

"No, I don't mind. Can't say it doesn't look good on you. Probably looks better on you than me," he teased.

A wide smile overtook her face as she was pleased to hear him say something that sounded like he was attracted to her. She finished making breakfast and brought their plates over to the table.

"How are you feeling?" Heather asked.

"Pretty good right now."

"You gave me a pretty good scare last night."

He laughed. "Probably gave myself a bigger one."

"Do you have many of them?"

"That was the first one. Hopefully, it's the last."

"Do you know why it happened?"

"I was shot in the head," Cain said bluntly.

"Oh my God."

"Yeah."

"What happened?" she asked, putting her hand on his arm.

"I can't really say. I don't remember anything about it. One day I just woke up in an army hospital with a bandage on my head and people telling me how lucky I was to survive."

"I can't even imagine what it was like. You seem like everything is fine."

"For the most part, it is. I feel healthy. My memory is gone though. I can't remember anything about my past. Names, faces, dates… it's all gone. I can't tell you anything about where I've been or what I've done before I woke up in that hospital," Cain explained, his eyes swelling up with tears. He wiped his eyes with the sleeve of his shirt to prevent him from crying.

"That's terrible. I feel so bad for you," Heather said, gushing. "Isn't there anything you can do to get your memory back?"

"Not that I know of. They say it might just come back one day out of the blue," he replied. "Or it might never come back again."

"Can't they bring in a family member or something? I've heard seeing a familiar face sometimes jogs people's memories."

"There isn't anybody."

"Nobody?"

"Well, I saw my file, and it seems I'm all there is.

Parents were killed and I have no other family to speak of."

"I'm so sorry," Heather said, rubbing his arm.

He gave her a warm smile that seemed to thank her for the comforting wishes without him saying a word. They continued talking as they ate, Heather feeling more connected to the man sitting next to her with each sentence he spoke. Even though she proclaimed she liked what she did, and the money was too good to pass up, she really yearned for a serious relationship. It was something she figured she'd never find in her line of work, at least not one worth having. She'd had a few boyfriends, but she knew they were mostly interested in her for the sex, and they thought it was cool to have a stripper for a girlfriend. Hardly the type of guys you brought home to mother. She could tell Cain was a different type of guy. One with standards and morals. That was obvious since he didn't ravage her the night before.

"What do you do for Sanders?" she asked.

"I don't think I'm supposed to tell you."

"Oh yeah. I forgot. Are you gonna be in New York for a while?"

"I don't know. I can live anywhere I want but I don't know where else I would go."

Cain got up from the table and put the dishes in the sink once the pair finished eating.

"That was really good, thank you. I really appreciate it."

"You're welcome. It was nice," Heather replied. "I enjoyed cooking for someone else for a change. Gets a little boring when you're only cooking for one all the time."

"That's surprising."

"Why is that surprising?"

"I dunno. I figured a girl like you would have guys banging down your door or begging at your feet to be with you," Cain surmised.

"A girl like me. You mean a stripper?" she asked without a hint of anger.

"No. I meant a girl as pretty as you."

"Oh. Well, there are plenty of guys banging down my door every day. But it doesn't mean anything. They're only after one thing."

"Sounds like you're not as into your profession as you made it seem last night."

"Well, I don't just go around talking about my feelings with everybody."

"Why are you talking about it now?" he asked.

"I don't know. I guess you're pretty easy to talk to," Heather admitted. "You're not like most guys I run into."

"I'll take that as a compliment."

"I meant it as one."

"So how long are you planning on staying? I mean, when do you have to get back to work or whatever?"

"Well, I told Sanders I'd stay for a couple of days to make sure you were OK," she said. "But if you don't want me to then I completely understand. I can leave whenever you want."

"It's fine."

"I can leave now. I'll just get dressed," she said as she got up from the table.

"Heather..."

"I mean, I really don't wanna feel like I'm imposing."

"Heather..."

"So, I'll just get dressed and then I'll be out of your hair."

"Heather..."

"I'll just tell Sanders you seem perfectly fine," she said nervously, not hearing anything Cain was saying.

"Heather," Cain yelled, finally succeeding in getting heard.

"What?"

"You can stay."

"I can?" she asked, surprised.

"Well, you already told Sanders you'd stay a couple days so you might as well. Plus, I'd like you to stay."

"You would?"

"Yeah. I mean, I told you I have memory issues. I forget how to cook," he joked.

A little sense of relief came over Heather as she never felt so comfortable and at ease with a man as she did with Cain. She was glad he wanted her to stay for a couple of days. She sauntered over to the couch in the living room, hoping to get a few lusty glances from him as she walked. Cain stood by the kitchen counter watching her every move. He couldn't remember much, but he was certain he hadn't seen legs that looked that nice in a long time. He sure didn't see anything like that in the army. He didn't feel right about having sex with her the minute he saw her but he felt no shame in undressing her with his eyes.

"I think you have one problem," he said.

"What's that?" she asked anxiously.

"If you're gonna be here a couple days, then I think you need your own clothes to wear. I mean, my shirt looks good on you but I don't think you can walk around the whole day like that."

"Don't bet on it."

Heather went to the bedroom and got dressed into her clothes from the night before. She came out about ten minutes later and told Cain she was going to her apartment to pack a few things.

"Want me to come with you?" Cain asked.

"Come with me? Why?" Heather asked, surprised by his request.

"Uh... I dunno. I thought maybe you'd need help or something."

"Umm, I think I should be OK."

She was a little reluctant at having Cain see her apartment. For the first time since she started stripping she seemed a little embarrassed about it. The only guys who'd been inside her apartment were guys she dated or paid for the privilege. For a few brief moments when they were talking at the table she felt like she was someone else. Like they were normal people just having a conversation and she kind of liked it. She'd hate for him to see her apartment and have the reality of her profession smack him in the face and change his opinion of her. She walked toward the door and thought about what might happen if he had another seizure while she was gone. She'd only be gone an hour or two but what if he had one and she wasn't there to help? What would Sanders say?

"I guess under the circumstances it'd be better off if you came with me," she reluctantly agreed. "I mean, with your seizures and all, I probably shouldn't leave you alone."

"Oh, yeah, you're probably right."

They took the elevator to the ground floor and walked out of the building. Almost immediately a beautiful blonde woman walked past them. She was rather tall with long hair and a striking figure. She gave Cain a slight smile. He was mesmerized by her and watched her walk past him. Heather noticed Cain continuing to watch the woman as she kept walking.

"I wish I'd gotten that kind of response from you last night," she deadpanned.

She expected some type of reply but he kept silent.

"I wasn't really serious," she said. "Most men would be falling over themselves if she walked past. I couldn't blame you."

After a minute, she realized she was basically talking to herself because he seemed like he was in another world. His head was still turned in that woman's direction though she was fading from view and barely noticeable at that point. Heather put her hand on his arm and shook it a little to try to break him from his trance. She shook it gently without success before putting a little more weight into it. It worked as he finally turned his head back to her. Heather was a little alarmed by the blank look that overtook his face.

"Are you OK?" she asked.

"Yeah, I'm fine."

"What's the matter? Don't remember seeing a pretty woman before?" she kidded.

"No. I mean, I saw something."

"What do you mean?"

"It was an image," Cain said.

"An image of what?"

"A woman."

The Cain Conspiracy

"Well, she just walked by you, it's understandable. Most men would probably have the same image in their head."

"No, it wasn't of her. It was somebody else."

"Who?"

"I don't know. I just saw her face. She had blonde hair, a little past her shoulders, and a pretty face."

"What was she doing?"

"Nothing. It was just her face. Everything else around her was just white space. Like a picture of a face on the pages of a book and that's all there is."

Heather could tell he seemed troubled by this vision. He seemed genuinely disturbed by it.

"I feel like I should know who it is. Like she's connected to me somehow," he said.

"Maybe it was a high school girlfriend or something. Maybe a friend that you knew from before."

"Maybe."

Heather made sure that Cain was all right before they started walking toward her apartment. They could've taken a cab, but they decided to walk the half hour to her place. It'd give them some time to talk along the way. With each step they took they seemed to grow a little closer to each other. In another time and place Heather thought about how things might be different. Maybe they'd be holding hands or exchanging playful glances with each other. But she knew that at this point in time there was no chance of anything ever developing further. After a half hour of walking, sidestepping bustling people who seemed to be charging at them, they arrived at a nice looking building that stretched up fifteen floors.

"I'm impressed," Cain said.

"I told you I was paid well."

They went inside and went up to her apartment on the eleventh floor. Heather put the key in and unlocked it, taking a deep breath before opening the door, hoping he wouldn't change his opinion of her after seeing it. There was nothing unordinary about the place, nothing that anyone would associate with her profession like poles attached to the ceiling, furry handcuffs on the couch or kinky fetishes. But to her, it was a stripper's place, and she attached a stigma to it even if no one else did.

"Well, here it is," she said, walking in.

"Very nice. I like it," Cain replied, looking around the living room. "Not quite what I expected."

"Which was?"

"Well, I, uh, I was kind of half expecting some unflattering things to be out and about."

"Most people do," she said dejectedly.

"Well, I'm gonna go pack a few things. Sit down and make yourself at home if you want. Kitchen's over there if you want a drink or anything."

Cain sat on the black leather couch, shifting around into different positions to get a feel for it. It was so comfortable that he didn't want to sit on it for too long or else he probably wouldn't want to get up. He walked into the kitchen and opened the refrigerator to see what was available. He poured a couple glasses of orange juice for the two of them. Just as he finished pouring there was a loud knock on the door.

"You want me to get that?" Cain asked.

"No, no," Heather huffed, scurrying into the room. "I'll get it."

She turned him around and told him to wait in the kitchen. The loud knocking continued.

"Come on, Heather, let's go," a deep voice yelled from the other side.

"Coming," she replied.

Heather opened the door to reveal a large, bald man with a Fu Manchu. She took a deep sigh, obviously displeased to see the heavyset man before her.

"Hi, Tommy," she said.

"So, what's this about you not working tonight?" he asked as he pushed past her.

"Sure, come on in," she said sarcastically.

"Why aren't you working? You don't look sick."

"I just feel like taking a couple of days off, OK?"

"Boss doesn't think that's a good idea."

"I don't really care what he thinks. I'm taking a few days," Heather insisted.

"Maybe you just need a little something to pick you up."

Tommy took some drugs out of his pocket and placed them down on the coffee table. Heather looked at him curiously before glancing down at the table.

"I don't know what you think you're doing but take that stuff and get out of here," she said.

"What, you don't have time for some old friends?" he asked cheerfully.

"Please, just leave."

Cain was still in the kitchen, listening to the entire conversation, and was beginning to worry about his new friend. She didn't sound particularly pleased to have him in her apartment and he didn't appear to be leaving anytime soon. He assumed she asked him to stay in the kitchen because she didn't want him to get involved in it. With each passing second of Tommy's bullying, Cain grew wearier of his presence. Another minute elapsed and Cain had heard all he could stomach. He couldn't stand bullies, especially when it was a woman involved. He emerged from the kitchen to the surprise of Tommy, who smiled as he looked over to Heather.

"Got a little something happenin' on the side, Heather?" he asked.

"Shut up," she replied.

"I believe the lady would like you to go," Cain said.

"She ain't no lady. Listen, buddy, just go back in the kitchen and mind your business," Tommy warned. "And maybe I won't bust you up some."

Cain didn't feel at all threatened by the burly man and continued to walk in his direction. Heather quickly looked at both of the men before her and tried to diffuse the situation before it got out of hand.

"Tommy, please just go," Heather said.

She put her hand on Tommy's arm to persuade him to leave but he shoved it aside. Cain kept walking closer to his adversary, who also wasn't about to back down. He looked like he was in good shape but Tommy had been pitted against plenty of guys who were in good shape but couldn't take the power of his punches.

"I really don't want to have an altercation with you," Cain told him. "But the lady asked you to go several times. I do believe it's best if you take her advice."

Tommy simply laughed at Cain's suggestion. He felt the implied threat Cain was giving him was just some tough guy bravado, and he didn't have the stones to back it up. Cain, on the other hand, was ready to toss the meathead out the door. He wasn't itching to fight, but could tell that the bald bruiser in front of him wouldn't have it any other way. Heather tried one more time to separate the pair, but it was falling on deaf ears.

"Matthew, please don't," she said.

"I'm not doing anything. If he leaves then there's no problem," Cain replied.

Heather looked up at him and sighed knowing there was nothing else she could do. She worried that one of them was going to get seriously hurt. She was fearful of Cain getting injured, and though she didn't personally care for Tommy, she didn't want Cain to get in any kind of trouble for anything he might do. Just as she turned around to face Tommy once more, he shoved her out of the way, pushing her into the wall. That gave Tommy the distraction he needed to catch Cain by surprise. He stunned Cain with a couple of big right hands, causing Cain to stumble backwards. After Cain regained his composure, he blocked a couple of Tommy's blows, countering with a few of his own. Cain quickly got the upper hand using a combination of strikes and kicks to get Tommy off balance. Cain unleashed some moves that he didn't even know he had in his arsenal. Now Tommy was the one trying to stave off his attacker, albeit unsuccessfully. Using a combination of punches, MMA holds, and kickboxing maneuvers, Cain had Tommy in a world of hurt. A few minutes of brutality elapsed with Cain showing no mercy on the thug lying before him. He bounced Tommy's head off the floor a few times with his punches.

Heather shook off the pain from hitting her head against the wall and watched as Cain continued his assault. Tommy was bleeding profusely from his nostrils, along with the bridge of it, which by now was broken. Blood was pouring out of cuts from above his right eye and both sides of his mouth. He coughed up a few teeth and was certain to lose consciousness any minute. Cain was showing no mercy and Heather was getting concerned about the carnage she was witnessing.

"Cain, stop!"

It was no use. She yelled a few more times for him to stop but he didn't hear a word of it. He was in such a zone that he had blocked everything out. There could've been trumpets playing behind him and he wouldn't have heard a single note. Heather worried that Cain was going to kill Tommy unless she stopped him. She was a little afraid of getting in the way and possibly catching some of Cain's wrath but felt she had no other choice. She raced in between the two men, catching hold of Cain's right arm in the process.

"Stop," she told him.

Cain immediately snapped out of whatever trance he was in, noticing the concerned look on her face. He released his curled up fist and dropped his arm, signaling the end of his confrontation. He slowly backed away, his face showing remorse for the amount of pain he just inflicted. He walked over to the window and reflected on what he'd just done. He was reminded of it by the blood stained on his knuckles. He was sure that Heather would think he was a monster now, and he wasn't sure if she'd be wrong. He realized he took it too far.

Heather had taken the next few minutes to get Tommy somewhat stable and help him back on his feet. She was sure he had some broken bones and probably a concussion. She wasn't really as concerned about his well-being since he was a major jerk, but didn't want anyone dying because of her. As soon as he was able to stand on his feet, she hurried him to the door to prevent any other problems. Not that Tommy was looking for anything since he now knew that his opponent could easily have killed him and was not close to being a match for him.

"You can consider yourself done," Tommy painfully whispered. "You'll never work again in this town as long as I can help it."

"Just go," Heather replied, shoving him out the door.

She knew he wasn't just giving an idle threat. He was connected to all the owners of the major clubs and would badmouth her to the point where she'd have to work in run down joints that hardly paid anything of substance. She closed the door behind him and sighed heavily as she wondered what she'd do now. Cain turned around to face her, somewhat shamefully, as he waited for her to snap at him. She looked at him a little differently now, seeing what was inside him, as opposed to just half an hour before that when it didn't seem like he was capable of such a vicious beating. Neither person said a word, both waiting for the other to start the conversation, as Heather slowly walked to the couch. She sat down, still not quite believing what she just witnessed. Cain could see the hesitation she now had with him and attempted to alleviate her fears.

"I, uh," he started. "I apologize."

Heather didn't respond. She wanted to, but just didn't know what to say. She leaned on her side, with her hand on her head, her arm being supported by the couch. She looked at him and could see how remorseful he was. He didn't look like a man who was proud of what he'd just done.

"If you're having second thoughts about anything, you don't have to worry," Cain said. "I'll let Sanders know I told you to stay away. He won't give you any problems."

"Sanders is the least of my problems now," she said with a laugh. "Tommy was right. He knows all the major players in this town. He'll make sure I don't work again. Looks like I'm unemployed now."

"I truly am sorry."

Cain was certain Heather didn't want to be near him anymore and started to make his way toward the door.

"Hey," Heather shouted.

"Yeah?" Cain replied, turning around.

"I really wasn't worried about him. I was worried about you."

"I wasn't in any danger."

"I know. That's what I was worried about. You made it look so easy."

Cain nodded and turned back around to head for the door. He put his hand on the knob before Heather stopped him again.

"Where are you going?" she asked.

"Back to my place."

"Aren't you forgetting something?"

"Like what?"

"Like me."

"You still..." Cain started to say.

"I'm not afraid of you," she responded, trying to calm his fears. "I know you were only trying to protect me. And I really am thankful and grateful for that."

Cain nodded in reply, not wanting to actually say words in response.

"The fact is that nobody's ever defended me like that before, or at all really," she stated. "It felt kind of good that you were there to protect me. I just got kind of scared at how far you were taking it."

"I guess once I got caught up in things..." Heather interrupted him before he could complete his thought.

"It's OK. You don't have to explain anything. Really, you don't."

"OK," he relented.

"I guess I saw what makes you so valuable to Sanders, huh?"

"I guess so."

"Where'd you learn all those moves?" she asked.

"To be honest, I have no idea. An hour ago I didn't even realize I could do some of those things."

"Well, just give me a few more minutes to pack and I'll be all ready," she said.

Heather went back into the bedroom to finish up as Cain sat down to wait for her. A few minutes later she emerged with a rolling suitcase and a duffel bag. As they left the apartment Heather wondered if she'd ever come back to it. She really didn't have many ties to it and intentionally kept the place devoid of too many personal items. They kept talking once they were in the cab as they drove back to Cain's apartment.

Heather sighed. "I hate all the traffic in this city."

"Isn't this normal?"

"Yeah, I suppose so. The Rangers play tonight so it's gonna be even worse since it's a playoff game."

"Oh."

"You like hockey?"

"Who? Me? I love hockey," Cain said. "That's a silly question. Why would you even ask that?"

"Have you even watched a game before?"

"Seriously? I feel a little insulted now," he joked. "Questioning my hockey knowledge."

"When was the last game you went to?" Heather insisted.

"Uh, well, you know, it's been a while."

"Who played?" she asked, smiling.

"It was, uh... the Rangers," he paused. "And the... Devils. The Devils, that's right."

"You have no idea, do you?"

"Well, you know... I have that whole memory thing going on right now."

They both looked at each other and burst out laughing.

"We should go to a game sometime," Heather said.

"Yeah. I'd like that."

Once they got back to Cain's apartment, Heather put some of her things away. Once she finished she went into the living room, sitting on a chair. Cain still felt bad about what transpired at her apartment and wondered what he could do to make it up to her.

"You know, I was thinking that maybe it's a good idea if you didn't go back to your apartment for a little while," Cain said.

"Why?"

"I dunno. Just in case your friends come back around for some reason. I'd feel better if you didn't go back."

"Where am I supposed to go?" she asked.

"Well, you could stay here for a few weeks."

"That's really nice of you... but I couldn't impose on you like that."

"You're not imposing. I'd like you to stay. Besides, it's kind of my fault about what happened. I wouldn't want to worry about you staying there by yourself."

"You'd worry about me?" Heather asked, a little amazed.

"Yeah. I would."

"Well, I guess I could stay a couple weeks. I mean, just until I get a new job and find a new place. Luckily I only have two months to go on the lease so I'm not losing out too much."

"So, if you can't keep, uh, doing what you're doing," Cain started, "then what're you gonna do? Move somewhere else?"

"I don't know. Maybe. Or maybe I'll actually try to find a real job. It's kinda scary not having a job."

"Well, like I said, you can stay here as long as it takes."

6

Sanders was in a meeting with his five deputy directors going over new files and information on possible targets. Every week they went over pertinent information about new targets or anything that was learned about targets they were actively seeking. Each director had a touch screen computer embedded in the oval table at his location, to which the information could be transferred and seen by everybody via a screen on the wall. Each deputy director was in charge of a different region which included North and South America, Europe, Asia, and Africa. Tim Wells, Deputy Director of South America passed a file over to Sanders and began going over the information, using the computer at his location.

"Mario Contreras," Wells began, as Contreras' name and picture popped up on the screen. "He's a guy who first popped up on our radar several months ago."

Also appearing on the screen was his list of offenses, physical description, marks or scars, aliases, and photos.

"This outstanding citizen is a Honduran national who was one of three men involved in the kidnapping, rape, and murder of a six-year-old girl in New York seven years ago. He was 23 at the time. It was planned as a ransom that went bad. The other two men were captured, sentenced, and are currently serving time in federal prison. Contreras, however, managed to avoid capture and disappeared without a trace. It was assumed he went back to South America, probably back to Honduras, though there was never any evidence to suggest that was so. Until last week," Wells continued, waiting for the photos on the screen to load. "These pictures were taken of Contreras in Honduras in the city of San Pedro Sula."

"What's the FBI's take on it, Tim?" Sanders asked.

"He was on their top ten for two years but they have no leads on him and he's seemingly falling off their radar. They have other fish to fry."

"Makes him a good target for us," Sanders mused.

"I was thinking it might make a good first assignment for Cain," Wells stated.

Sanders stared at the screen, only taking his eyes off it to look at Wells momentarily, his fingers stroking his chin, deep in thought.

"I agree," Sanders finally said. "Hand the file over to Shelly and have her work out the details with Cain."

"Right."

"What else you got?"

Wells spent the next half hour going over various forms of information he'd received, not all of it deemed reliable or anything that could be acted upon soon. Anything that was agreed on to be relevant was saved for future use so they could acquire more information or scheduled to be handed out to a handler. Once the meeting ended, Wells went back to his office and emailed the entire contents of the Contreras file to Shelly Lawson. All handlers got automatic text messages when they received emails so any new information or cases were handled promptly.

Lawson was in a small coffee shop when she got the text alerting her to a new email. She was going over logistics of a mission of another agent when she logged onto her tablet to check the email's contents. As an agency, Contreras was usually not the kind of target that they went after. He was not a threat to the safety and security of the United States, which was their primary goal. But he was the perpetrator of a major crime that escaped punishment, which they sometimes decided worthy of pursuing if time allowed and it could be done quickly. They also usually picked these cases for new agents to get them acclimated to the agency and how things were done. Lawson began working immediately on the file and quickly engulfed herself on the contents. While working on it she decided to give Cain a heads up to let him know a mission was coming his way so he could start mentally preparing for it. She took her phone out of her purse and dialed his number.

"How you feeling?" Lawson asked.

"OK, I guess."

"Getting tired and bored of sitting there?"

"A little bit," he replied.

"Well, looks like that'll be ending soon."

"Why's that?"

"You're being given a mission."

"Where?"

"Honduras," she said.

"What's the target?"

"I'll go over everything with you tomorrow. Come into the Center at ten o'clock and I'll give you the details. I'm still working things out right now."

"I'll be there."

Cain walked into the Center at 9:55, greeting the receptionist, before swiping his card to go through the door located in the back. He was greeted by Lawson.

"Anxious or excited?" she asked.

"Neither, really," Cain solemnly said.

They took the elevator up to the fourth floor to go to Lawson's office. Almost all offices in the building were surrounded by glass except for the director, deputy directors, and offices used for special purposes such as interviewing or interrogation. They sat down at her desk and she handed him copies of all the information she had about the case. Cain opened the folder and started reading the file.

"When do I leave?" Cain asked.

"Tomorrow. Your plane ticket's in there."

Cain looked in the back of the folder and took the ticket out, holding it up, looking at both sides of it. He looked somewhat confused.

"There's no return ticket?" he asked.

"It's up to you to purchase one to get back once the mission's been completed. We don't like to rush our agents into making decisions that aren't in their best interests just so they can catch a plane. Take your time to do it right and come back when you're done. You'll fly down to Miami from JFK here in New York and take a connecting flight to Honduras from there on American

Airlines. Your flight from JFK is 2:00pm on Monday. Should take a little over six hours to get there. With the two-hour time difference you should be there around seven."

"What do you want me to do when I get him?"

"Eliminate him. He's not to be taken, captured, or transported. We only work one way."

"Dead," Cain said.

"Other agencies worry about capturing and all that stuff."

"Too much red tape?"

"Take him out and it's done. That simple."

"How will I know where to find Contreras?"

"You'll be flying into the Ramon Villeda Morales International Airport, which is about seven miles outside of San Pedro Sula. Once you arrive, you'll be greeted by a man named Javier Ruiz. He'll update you on the situation when you arrive."

"Why not just have this Ruiz take care of it then if he's already there?" Cain asked.

"Because he's not trained to eliminate targets. He lives and works there and feeds us information. We can't have locals doing the jobs themselves and risk compromising them," Lawson said.

"Is this Ruiz trustworthy?"

"Very. We've worked with him before. He's very reliable. There are absolutely no issues with that. Once you arrive, Ruiz will supply you with whatever weapons you need."

"I'm going unarmed?"

"While it is possible to get a gun through security, there's no need to take risks when you can be supplied with one as soon as you touch ground. But I do suggest obtaining a weapon be your first priority once you arrive."

"Why's that?"

"Because Honduras has the highest murder rate in the world and is one of the poorest countries in Latin America. Crime is widespread and foreigners are deemed to be wealthy and frequently targeted. In the last 17 years there have been 113 U.S. citizens murdered there with only 29 resolved cases. There are roughly three murders in that city alone every day. Be aware of driving at night as carjacking is prevalent, as well as crimes of opportunity."

"Great. I'm excited already," Cain deadpanned.

"Contreras has been seen in the tourist city of San Pedro Sula which has seen armed robberies against cars traveling from the airport, most likely on tips received from someone working at the airport. Several citizens have been murdered shortly after arriving so it's quite possible you'll be targeted as soon as you arrive."

"And I'm not going armed?" Cain asked sarcastically.

"You'll be fine. Don't worry," Lawson replied.

"Oh, yeah, can't see any reason why I wouldn't be."

"Also, don't drink the water."

"And I thought that was just a bad punchline."

"They lack the substantial infrastructure to maintain water purity so only buy bottled water," she continued. "I also wouldn't eat any raw fish, fruit, or vegetables."

"Right."

"Hot foods, fresh bread, coffee, tea, beer, and dry food like crackers are usually fine to eat."

"Well, that's encouraging."

"Assuming you don't get them from street vendors," she said, smiling.

"Wow, this is a regular vacation destination."

"Remember, the sooner you get it done, the sooner you get home."

"These are the photos of Contreras that were taken of him last week," Lawson said, putting them down on the desk. "And just in case you have second thoughts about killing him, this is the photo of the little girl he raped and killed."

Cain stared at Lawson for a few seconds before putting his eyes on the picture of the little girl. He picked the photo up, and focused on it, her image burned into his mind.

"It'll be done," Cain stated plainly.

After leaving the Center, Cain went back to his apartment. Heather was already in the kitchen preparing lunch for them.

"You know, I was thinking about getting tickets for the Rangers game on Tuesday. What do you think?" Heather asked.

"Umm... I'm gonna have to take a rain check on it," he regretfully replied. "I'm going out of town for a few days."

"Oh," she said, a hint of disappointment showing in her voice. "For your work?"

"Yeah."

"Where are you going?"

"I can't really say. It shouldn't take long though. I should be back in a couple days."

"OK. Well, I hope you have a good trip."

Cain sat down at the table as Heather continued

making their lunch. She brought over a couple of turkey sandwiches, chips, and sodas for the both of them.

"So, when are you leaving?" Heather asked.

"Monday."

They ate in silence for a few minutes, neither able to figure out the right words to say. Cain could tell she seemed uneasy about something, though he wasn't sure what it was.

"Are you gonna be OK here by yourself for a few days?" Cain asked.

"Yeah, I'll be fine."

"Are you sure? Because I could try to get someone to come stay with you while I'm gone."

"Really? You're acting like I'm in witness protection or something. I've been living on my own for a few years now. I think I'll be fine a few days without you."

"Sorry. I guess I've got that whole protecting thing going on," he said.

"It's OK. It's cute. Besides, you leaving will help me out, anyway."

"How's that?"

"I won't have to look after you," she kidded. "I'll be able to spend a lot of time job hunting. I'll just check out Monster and some other job sites. Hopefully, I'll find a few things."

"I'm sure you will. At least you have a degree. That'll help."

"Yeah, but the gap on my resume won't help too much."

"What gap?" Cain asked.

"Well, I don't think that putting down stripping and

other extracurricular activities on my resume will do much for my job chances."

"I see your point."

"I thought you might."

"Then don't put that down," Cain said.

"I have to put down something. If I don't, they're gonna ask what I've been doing the last few years."

"How about you just put down you had your own business?"

"My own business?" Heather asked.

"Well, it kinda is, isn't it?"

"And just what kind of business have I been running?"

He smiled. "Entertainment."

They spent a couple of days polishing up Heather's resume. It'd been several years since she sent a resume out to anyone so she was grateful for his help. Cain enjoyed helping her even if he wasn't sure he was doing much good. He'd been in the army since graduating high school so he was fairly certain he'd never written one himself. The rest of the weekend they spent just trying to get to know each other. Cain was intrigued by the life of the beautiful woman he was now sharing an apartment with. Another place and time he might've made a move on her but he didn't think it was the appropriate time to do that. At least not until he was more certain of how his life as an agent would be. He knew there was going to be a good amount of travel involved and wasn't sure it'd be fair to make someone wait for him, not knowing when he'd be coming home.

Heather tried grilling Cain on his past to get a better idea of his life but he didn't divulge much. Not because he didn't want to but because he had no answers. He really didn't know what he liked or things he tried before. He tried to deflect most of her questions to avoid making it seem like he was trying to hide something from her.

The morning that Cain was supposed to leave on his trip he got up early, not able to sleep. He tossed and turned most of the night thinking about what it might be like. A lot of thoughts crossed his mind, knowing full well that it probably wouldn't be like anything he had envisioned. He tried to eat breakfast but only had a few bites as his stomach was too nervous to put any food into it. Cain was trying not to make too much noise so he wouldn't wake Heather, but she eventually walked out from the bedroom, anyway.

"I'm sorry," Cain said, noticing her standing in the door.

"For what?"

"Waking you up. I was trying to be quiet."

"No, it wasn't you. I just had to go to the bathroom and noticed that you were up," she said.

"Oh."

"I guess you're leaving soon?"

"Yeah, in a few minutes," Cain replied.

"I figured so. I'll make sure everything's good here."

"Oh, I know you will. I don't have any worries about it."

"Good," she said.

"Well, I should be going."

"You take care of yourself."

"I will."

Heather walked closer to him, trying to get a read on the situation. She really wanted to give him a hug but wasn't sure if he would push her away. She decided to go for it and awkwardly put her arms around him, barely touching each other. She wasn't sure what it was about Cain that made her so careful about both of their feelings as she'd never acted so gingerly around a man before. Maybe it was because of her past that she wanted to become a different person. Part of that transformation would include being more sensitive to her feelings. Heather assumed that when Cain looked at her, he still saw a stripper and she'd have to work at changing that perception. She knew that wouldn't happen overnight and that it'd take time. It would also take her being patient and not trying to force him into wanting her. She realized that if she tried to force herself onto him that it might make him think twice about her and back away. If she was ever able to get him to look past her background, it'd have to be a realization that came to him on his own.

7

Cain was walking through the Ramon Villeda Morales International Airport looking for the rendezvous point. He was instructed to meet his contact at a table in front of a Wendy's. Ruiz would be wearing a black New York Yankees baseball hat. It only took a few minutes before Cain located him. Ruiz was eating a Baconator as Cain approached. Cain sat across from him as Ruiz grabbed a napkin to get the grease off his hand, shaking Cain's as they introduced themselves.

"Ruiz?"

"Mr. Cain, pleasure to meet you," Ruiz replied.

"Your English is better than I anticipated."

"I speak it fluently. I owe it all to Rosetta Stone. Whoever made that program is a genius. I also speak French, Spanish, Russian, and German. Right now, I am studying Chinese."

"That's impressive. I still struggle with English," Cain joked.

"Can I get you something?"

"No. Thank you."

"Have you done this before?" Ruiz asked.

Cain stared at him momentarily, wondering if he should be truthful or lie about his experience. He didn't know the man sitting across from him, or know if his answer would make a difference in his help.

"This is my first assignment," Cain said.

Cain figured it was best to just be truthful. The agency trusted Ruiz, so he had no reason to doubt them. He looked around, surveying the airport, as Ruiz finished his dinner.

"You will do fine. I have good instincts for these things," Ruiz said.

"I believe you have some information for me," Cain said.

Ruiz nodded as he finished chewing. "I do. I have a rental car for you outside. I have the information you need in there."

"Good."

Cain followed Ruiz through the airport as they made their way to the car. Once inside Ruiz handed Cain a black duffel bag. Cain opened it, finding a file folder, as well as a sniper rifle and a Glock pistol. Cain began looking through the folder as Ruiz started driving.

"Where are we going first?" Cain asked.

"I'll take you to your hotel. You have a very nice room at the Hilton Princess. This way you can relax tonight after your journey plus map out your strategy."

"Very nice."

They'd been driving for about ten minutes on the highway when Ruiz spotted a white car following them.

"Get ready, my friend," Ruiz said.

"Why? What's going on?"

"I think we're about to have company."

The white car sped around them, then slowed down in front of them as a maroon-colored car took position behind them.

"We're being boxed in," Cain said.

"They most likely just want money."

The three cars slowly drifted to the side of the road, all of them eventually coming to a stop. Cain reached into the bag, slowly removing the Glock and putting it down by his side to conceal it. Cain's heart was racing as he waited for their visitors to make their move. He started sweating, anxious and nervous, hoping he'd make the right move. Two men got out of the car in front of them and started walking back to them. Cain noticed they both were carrying a gun in their hands. He checked the rearview mirror and saw two more getting out of the car behind them. They also had guns and started walking toward the rental. Cain put his finger on the trigger as he waited for the right moment. Two men stood near the bumper of their car as the other two stood by the driver and passenger side windows.

"Money," said the one by Ruiz.

Ruiz turned his head to look at Cain, not sure if he should comply with the demands or wait for Cain to make his move. Cain suddenly raised his pistol to the man by his window, blowing a hole through the man's chest. He then spun around and fired a shot past Ruiz, surprising their attacker before he could respond, fatally hitting him in the chest. Cain opened his door, jumping out onto the ground, firing a couple more shots. His target dropped to the ground, writhing in pain, the bullets lodging in his thigh and stomach. The other man ran back to the maroon car and sped off. Cain jumped up and steadied his aim as the man drove past. He was ready to fire but didn't have a clear shot and let him go. He walked closer to the wounded man on the ground to check on his status. He wasn't sure if the wounds were life threatening but Cain was beyond angry and the rush he felt overtook him. He aimed his gun at the man's chest and pulled the trigger, quickly ending the man's pain. Cain retreated back to the car, eager to move before police or witnesses showed up. As soon as he got in, Ruiz sped away.

"That was amazing," an overexcited Ruiz said. "Oh my goodness. Any doubts I had before are all gone now, my friend."

"Nice," Cain replied, putting the gun back in the bag. He sighed, amazed himself over what he'd just done.

They had a nice, quiet drive the rest of the way to the hotel. Ruiz grabbed Cain's luggage as Cain carried the duffel bag inside. He was led up to his executive room, Cain impressed at how lavish it looked. It was a very spacious room with a king-sized bed and marble bathroom. The men put Cain's bags down on the bed, Cain then checking out the view from the double wide windows.

"So, how'd you get involved in all this?" Cain asked.

"Me? It's a long story."

"I hope you get paid well."

"I do get paid well. But money is only secondary for me. It is not the reason I do this," Ruiz said.

"What is?"

Ruiz sat on the bed and took his hat off as he thought

about the events that led him to this moment. He was a middle-aged man, probably in his late forties, who was bearing some emotional scars. The pain was evident on his face.

"It was about twelve years ago. One day I get a phone call from the police. They tell me my 16-year-old daughter had been raped and murdered. They had no suspects and no leads. The killers went free," Ruiz said.

"I'm sorry for your loss."

"I started trying to find out on my own but I got nowhere. No one would talk to me and everywhere I went the information got cold. Then one day I learned there were U.S. officials in the area on business. I went to them for help but they all refused. All except for one. He was a CIA officer and agreed to look into it. One week later he informed me he found my daughter's killer. It turned out to be a police official's son, and they were covering up the incident. He then contacted officials in our government and her killer was brought to justice. He was eventually executed for his crime. I owed this man for what he had done for me."

"I'm sure it wasn't easy for you and your wife," Cain said.

"I have no wife. We were eighteen when we had Maira. We were very young. She did not even want the baby once we found out. But, luckily, I convinced her that it was the right thing; even if she did not want the child that I would raise the baby on my own. She agreed. She stayed for a few months after Maira was born. One night while we slept she left, never to return."

"That's pretty tough."

"I shed no tears. She didn't want to be a mother, and it

was best that she left before Maira grew up to see the person that she was."

"Well, sorry to hear it," Cain said, sympathizing. "Still, lucky for you that CIA officer showed up."

"Yes. You will enjoy working for him. He is a good man."

"I will? Who are you talking about?"

"Ed Sanders, of course," Ruiz said. "He is now your employer, is he not?"

"He is," Cain said.

"Several years later he contacted me once more asking to work with him again and he would pay me for my services. But payment is not what makes me do this. What makes me do this is justice. Bad men paying the price for their sins is what I do this for."

"I understand. Is this all that you do?"

"I have my own business. We export products such as coffee and cigars. I do not get wealthy off this but we make a profit. Along with what I get paid from your people, I do all right for myself."

Ruiz watched Cain as he continued looking out the window, trying to analyze him.

"You seem different than previous men I have worked with."

"How's that?" Cain asked.

"I am not sure yet. There is just something different with you."

"Well, when you figure it out, you let me know."

"I will do that," Ruiz said. "Now, let's get down to business."

Ruiz got the folder out of the duffel bag and took it over to the large desk against the wall. Cain walked over and sat down, examining the contents of the folder. There were pictures of Contreras in different spots around town over the previous two weeks along with information on where he'd been visiting.

"Who are some of these men he's been seen with?" Cain asked.

"I have not been able to capture the identities of these men. It is a mystery to this point."

Contreras had been photographed having discussions with several different men. Ruiz thought these men looked like they were European. These were new pictures that Cain hadn't been shown before.

"What would he be doing meeting with Europeans?" Cain asked.

"That is the question," Ruiz said. "When will you go after him?"

"I'll start looking for him tomorrow."

"Then you will most likely find him."

"Why's that?"

"The last few weeks I have observed him eating lunch at Applebee's three days a week. Always arrives between twelve and one."

"Seriously? Applebee's?"

"What is wrong?"

"I just wouldn't picture a criminal from Honduras being addicted to an American restaurant chain."

"Yes, well, I suppose he enjoys the hamburgers, perhaps?"

"I guess so."

"He usually eats on the patio so that should give you a good visual on him."

They talked for the next hour about their target,

discussing all the places Contreras had been. He was seen at Central Park, City Mall, The Francisco Saybe Theatre, The Old Train Station, and the San Pedro Sula Cathedral. All were within two miles of his hotel. They reviewed the dates and times, as well as who he met with, to see if there were any patterns. Almost all of the meetings he had occurred between twelve and four and none appeared to be with locals. Everyone Contreras met with was a foreigner. Cain and Ruiz finalized their plans before Ruiz left for the evening.

"Meet me for lunch at Applebee's tomorrow?" Cain asked.

"You think that's wise for us to be there with him?"

"Well, if he's by himself, it won't matter after a few minutes," Cain said. "And if he's with someone else, then I want to see who it is. Plus, we'll blend right in. I'll stand out more if I'm by myself. They don't know who we are, anyway."

A few minutes after Ruiz left the hotel, Cain called Lawson to update her on the developments.

"How's it going so far?" she asked.

"Fantastic. Killed three men so far."

"What?!"

"And the day's not even over yet."

"What happened?"

"They tried to hijack us on the way to the hotel."

"Are you in trouble?" she asked.

"No. No witnesses."

"Good. What else can I do for you?"

"I've got some pictures of Contreras meeting with a few people," Cain said.

"Send them over to me and I'll have them analyzed."

"Sending them now."

"I'll call you back in an hour or two."

Cain took photos of the pictures and uploaded them to his computer, then sent them to Lawson. He decided to lay down on the bed while he waited for a return call just to relax since he was still pretty jacked up from all the commotion in getting there. He closed his eyes and relived every second of the killings, from the moment he pulled the gun out of the duffel bag, waiting for his would-be victims. He surprised himself at how easily it came to him. There was no hesitation in his actions. He then imagined what it would be like killing Contreras. He envisioned Contreras sitting down to eat, Cain looking on from a distance in some window, then watching him drop to the ground after he pulled the trigger. Cain somehow stopped thinking of the gruesome images for a few minutes and dozed off. He was awakened two hours later by the ringer of his cell phone going off. It was Lawson.

"Hey," Cain answered.

"We've run some analysis on the three men in your photos."

"And?"

"We came up empty. We checked all our databases, ran them through our facial recognition software, and contacted a few people who might be in the know. Everything came back negative. Which means they're either insignificant players or they're low level guys, meeting with Contreras on someone else's behalf."

"So, do I still take him out?"

"Yes, but follow him for a couple of days. See if he meets with anyone else first. Him meeting with foreigners could indicate he's on the verge of something we aren't aware of and we'd like to know what that is if possible. Take pictures of anyone else he comes in contact with."

"OK. Will do."

Cain closed his eyes again, hoping to fall asleep quickly, knowing he could have an action-packed itinerary the following day. He turned his head from side to side as strange images started appearing. The blonde-haired woman from before popped up again. The first few images were like before, just her head floating around as if it were trapped in a television screen. Then her whole body appeared, wearing a red dress, walking down a busy street. She kept turning back as if she were looking for him. She then ducked into a store where he lost track of her. He opened his eyes, wiped the sweat off his forehead, and sat up in bed. He knew this woman must've been important to him at some point in his life. It couldn't have been just some random person he kept imagining. Cain took a few seconds to clear his head before lying back down. This time his mind was clear, and he fell asleep within a few minutes, no visions clouding his head.

8

Cain woke up early the next morning, around six o'clock, and immediately called for room service. He ate fairly quickly and decided to take a walk around, seeing some of the sights for himself. He grabbed the Glock pistol and tucked it in the back of his belt before leaving his room. He walked to each of the places Contreras had been seen to get an idea of his sight lines. At each location, he carefully looked around to see where he'd be able to set up shop as well as where he could position himself depending on where Contreras was. Cain spent the good part of the morning scouting out those locations, but he also walked around the area, just to see if there were any other spots he would be able to bury himself in. Once he saw it was eleven o'clock, he walked over to the Applebee's and waited for Ruiz to show up. He figured it was better to show up early in the event Contreras didn't stop by at his usual time. Cain grabbed one of the tables at the back of the patio, giving him a good observation point to see every other table out there. Ruiz came by five minutes to noon, still wearing his Yankees hat.

"You wear that everywhere you go?" Cain kidded.

"It's my good luck hat."

"I hope it is."

They sat and talked for a few minutes, waiting and hoping for Contreras to show his face. Cain was genuinely interested in the Honduran culture and what it was like to live there.

"This is a great place to be," Ruiz said. "Beautiful weather, good people, excellent food."

"Lots of murder."

"You are right, unfortunately, there is very high murder rate here. But is that so much unlike any of your American big cities like New York or Los Angeles? Crime is widespread in this world no matter the location. That is why we must not fail in our work here. To protect our children and make it safer for them."

"I suppose you're right."

Luckily for them their wait didn't last very long. Twenty minutes after twelve, Contreras walked into the restaurant, getting a table a couple rows in front of the American and his companion. With his sunglasses still on, Cain turned his head slightly to give the appearance he was looking elsewhere, but still kept his eyes glued to Contreras' table. Contreras appeared to be eating alone at first, as he ordered his food, but ten minutes later his company arrived. Two men sat at the table and also ordered food. They brought a briefcase and set it down in front of them. They took out some papers and handed them to Contreras who studied them carefully, occasionally stopping to take a drink. Cain could see Contreras' head nodding, without saying anything, appearing to like what he was reading. Cain took out his cell phone and pretended to be texting, carefully positioning the phone to get a good picture of the three men seated in front of him. He was able to get a few pictures of the unknown individuals, a full face shot of the one, and a side shot of the other. Contreras had his back to the camera, but he was not important since he was already known. Cain sent the images to Shelly Lawson, letting her know the meeting was taking place right at that moment.

"Will analyze immediately," Lawson texted back. "Stay with them."

"Will do," Cain responded.

Cain and Ruiz kept talking as they ate their lunch, making it appear they were just regular people. Cain continued keeping an eye on the Contreras table in the process. Contreras was doing a lot of talking, and moving his hands around frequently, making it seem like he was incensed about something. Unfortunately, Cain wasn't good at lip reading, and couldn't even make a guess at what was being discussed. The other two men appeared to be staying calm, and not saying a whole lot, making it seem like maybe it was just something Contreras was passionate talking about. Cain did notice that the one man seemed to do most of the talking for the pair when they did speak, his partner mostly listening and looking around occasionally. As Cain studied the man, he came to the conclusion that he must've been a bodyguard. He figured someone in a higher authority would've had more to say. The fact he kept looking around made it seem like he was keeping an eye out for trouble. Both parties stayed at their tables until a little after one. Contreras concluded his meeting by shaking the hands of both his visitors, who left their briefcase behind as they walked away from the table.

"Should we follow them?" Ruiz asked.

"No. My target is Contreras," Cain replied. "Seems like something's going on, but we don't know who they are yet. Could be nobody."

"You are right, of course."

The briefcase changed Cain's plans slightly. Before, he was planning on killing Contreras with a sniper rifle. Now, he was thinking about what might be in that briefcase. If he took Contreras out up close, he could quickly snatch the briefcase. If he killed him from afar, he likely wouldn't have time to take it with onlookers and police converging on the dead body.

"Are you going to do it now?" Ruiz asked.

"Too many witnesses here."

About ten minutes later Contreras paid his bill and left the restaurant, briefcase in hand. Cain and Ruiz followed him out the door, watching him get into the back seat of a car, which then drove off.

"Damn," Cain said.

"What is wrong?"

"I walked here."

"We can take my car," Ruiz offered.

They raced over to his car and followed Contreras. It was a short chase as the Contreras car stopped a few minutes later in front of a cathedral. Contreras got out with his briefcase and walked inside. Ruiz parked his car in front as Cain debated going inside as well. He decided to wait until Contreras returned before either killing him or continuing following him. A half hour passed with no sign of Contreras, causing Cain to get a little worried that he knew he was being followed and ducked out somewhere. His driver was still parked in front, though, so Cain thought maybe Contreras was having another meeting inside with someone. It'd be a perfect place to have a meeting without having wandering eyes looking down at them. Patience wasn't Cain's strongest attribute, and he'd just about exhausted however much he had of it. He told Ruiz to wait for him to get back and exited the car.

Cain entered the cathedral and looked around, trying to spot Contreras. He started walking along the wall, spotting Contreras a few rows near the back, on the right-hand side near the end of a pew. He was sitting by himself, his head looking down, seeming to be in prayer. Cain quietly walked toward him, hoping he wouldn't notice him coming. He walked into the pew behind Contreras, sliding to the end, sitting directly behind him. Contreras, feeling the presence of someone behind him, slowly picked his head up.

"What can I do for you?" Contreras asked.

"There's not a thing you can do for me."

"Then why are you here? For the prayers?"

"I'm like a courier. Just here to deliver a message," Cain said.

"I'm listening."

"Where's the briefcase?" Cain asked, not seeing it next to Contreras.

"I don't see how that's of any importance to you."

"Who were you just meeting with?"

"Once again, I don't see how that is important to you."

"Well, in the grand scheme of things it really doesn't matter 'cause it's not gonna change your fate."

"Which is what?"

"You're dead."

"If you're planning to kill me, you could at least tell me why or who sent you," Contreras said, trying to buy time to think of a way out of his situation.

"There was a little girl in New York a few years ago that you sent to an early grave," Cain said.

"This is about that?" Contreras responded with a laugh. "Please, tell me how much they are paying you to do this and I'll double it for you to walk away. I'll put you on my payroll as we speak. I have big plans coming."

"No thanks."

Cain withdrew his gun from his belt, ready to put an end to Contreras' life. Just as he started to raise the pistol, Contreras slumped forward, part of his head exploding, pieces flying everywhere. Blood splattered onto Cain, who ducked for cover. Whoever killed him used a silencer since there was no sound from the shot being fired. Cain peeked over the pew, looking for the man who took out his target. He carefully raised his head above the pew, not wanting to expose himself too much in case the shooter intended to take him out as well. After being stationary for a minute, Cain assumed the shooter already left, and he raced toward the door. He wanted to quickly get out of there before police arrived.

As soon as Cain went through the door, he noticed a man getting out of the passenger side of Contreras' car. The man was holding a brown briefcase which looked like the same one Contreras had in his possession. He was a white man, about average height, short brown hair, and had a goatee. Once the man closed the car door, he looked around and noticed Cain standing at the cathedral's doors. The man smiled as Cain started running toward him. A car squealed its brakes as it rushed to the curb, the man getting in the back seat, rushing off before Cain got there. Cain slapped his leg in disgust, not believing what just happened. He walked over to Contreras' car and peered through the window. The driver was dead, as Cain assumed he would be, slumped to his side, his head resting against the window. He rushed over to Ruiz's car before anyone realized what happened and the pair drove away.

"What just happened?" Ruiz asked.

"I wish I knew."

"Is Contreras dead?"

"Yeah."

"The mission was successful then, no?"

"I'm not the one who killed him," Cain said, displeased.

"Oh. If you did not kill him, then who did?"

"That's the question."

"And why?"

Ruiz drove Cain back to the Hilton Princess so Cain could contact Lawson and figure out his next step. Cain thanked Ruiz for his help and told him he'd contact him if he needed anything else.

"Good luck, my friend, it's been a pleasure," Ruiz said.

"Same to you."

Cain went straight to his room and immediately called Lawson.

"Hey, we're still working on identifying the men in the photos," Lawson said.

"Contreras is dead."

"Oh. OK. A little faster than I anticipated, but that's OK."

"Except I didn't do it," Cain said.

"Then who did?"

"I don't know. I was about to and someone took a shot from behind me and blew his head off."

"Did you get a look at him?"

"Yeah, but he wasn't one of the guys from the pictures."

"Well, this is an interesting development, isn't it?" Lawson said.

"If you say so."

"We certainly didn't anticipate any complications on this mission."

"You're telling me."

"Well, sit tight until you hear back from me."

An hour went by without a word from Lawson. Cain took a shower then had food sent up to his room. As he sat down to eat, the phone in his room started ringing. A strange look came across him as he didn't know who'd be calling him there. He cautiously walked over to it, almost like he was afraid it might blow up, and after a few rings picked it up.

"Hello," Cain said.

"Mr. Mathews, we have an outside call for you, do you accept the call?" the front desk asked.

"Yeah."

"One moment."

"So, the room's registered to a Michael Mathews, is that your real name?" the mysterious man asked.

"Who's this?"

"Have you forgotten me so soon?"

"Who are you? You know my name, it's only fair that I know yours."

"Fair point. My name's George Wentworth. I'm sorry about interrupting your meeting at the church. It looked like it was about to end but I needed to be the one who finished it."

"Why was it so important that you needed to do it?"

"That's what I'm paid for," the man said.

"Who are you working for?"

"That's nothing for you to be concerned with."

"What was in the briefcase?"

"I don't know. I was just instructed to get it. What was inside was not my business."

"Are you with Specter?" Cain asked, not sure if he should've said the name, but he was curious if it was another test by Sanders.

"Specter? Ah, so you're a Project Specter agent," Wentworth said. "Now that makes it all the more interesting. That means Mathews probably isn't your real name."

"The same as Wentworth probably isn't yours. What do you know about Specter?"

"I was once in that boat, as you are now."

"You were an agent?"

"Yes. For several years. Now, I'm in business for myself. I freelance. Who is your handler?"

"Shelly Lawson."

"Shelly? She was my handler also. I loved Shelly. She was the only difficult part about leaving. If Shelly's your handler then you're in good hands. She'll take care of you."

"She seems like she knows her stuff," Cain said.

"Oh, she does. There's no one better. Just a word of advice from one agent to another; be careful."

"Of what?"

"Everything. Don't trust everything that's said or done," Wentworth added. "I don't know your particular situation but everything they tell you is not necessarily the truth or as it appears. They have their own agenda for things. They will play you for their own advantage. The same as if you're playing with fire... be cautious around it."

"Thanks for the tip. Maybe we'll run into each other again someday."

"If you're with Project Specter, it's more than likely."

"How'd you know where I was, anyway?" Cain asked.

"I followed you after the church. I wanted to see who the mysterious man was that I was competing with," Wentworth replied. "Some more advice for you, always make sure you're not being followed."

"I'll do that next time."

"You do that. Well, I have to go. Until next time."

Cain picked up his phone, ready to call Lawson, but put it back down. He figured she'd be calling him soon enough. He sat down to finish the rest of his dinner as he replayed the conversation with Wentworth in his mind. Just as Cain finished dinner his phone rang. It was Lawson.

"Looks like we got some hits on those pictures you took," Lawson said.

"What's the word?"

"The men Contreras was meeting with were definitely European, specifically Russian. The man he was talking to was Andrei Kurylenko. He is a burgeoning international arms dealer. He's been making contacts all over the world. He's someone we'll be having to contend with shortly. The other man with him was one of his top aides, Dmitri Butsayev."

"That seems like bad news."

"It is. If Contreras was meeting with Kurylenko that can only mean that Contreras was trying to acquire massive amounts of firearms."

"That doesn't seem like that was part of his repertoire," Cain said.

"Contreras dropped off the map after New York. He must've been trying to step up his notoriety."

"He did say he had big plans coming up."

"Kurylenko must've been what he had in mind," Lawson said.

"If Contreras was trying to get weapons then why would Kurylenko have him killed?"

"Maybe they disagreed on terms. Or maybe it wasn't Kurylenko."

"Who else would it be?" Cain asked.

"It's tough to say. We don't know exactly what else Contreras was into."

"So, what do you want me to do next?"

"Go home. Stay there for another day and relax. If you're able to pick up anything then all the better. If not, then come back on Thursday until we get another mission mapped out for you."

"OK," Cain replied, wondering if he should tell her about his conversation with Wentworth.

"Have anything else for me?" Lawson asked.

"Umm."

"What is it?" she asked.

"I dunno."

"C'mon, what is it? You can say anything to me. It's OK. If it's private, then I'll just keep it between us. You can trust me."

"Well, it's about the man who killed Contreras," Cain said.

"I've been checking on it. I've been checking into known violent people on our radar who arrived in Honduras the previous few days but so far, we've come up empty. Whoever it was must've slipped in quietly."

"I already know who it is."

"You do? How? That's good work by you but how did you find out already?"

"He called me."

"What do you mean he called you?"

"Apparently, he followed me to my hotel and called my room," Cain said.

"Well, that's highly unusual. What did he have to say?"

"He said he wanted to see who I was."

"And did you tell him?" Lawson asked.

"Just the cover name I was using."

"Good."

"I thought maybe he was from Specter, that it was another test for me."

"Absolutely not. I would know if it was."

"He said he was," he said.

"That's impossible. We have no other agents in that area. I would know if we did."

"He said he was a former agent who is now freelancing."

"I'm gonna have to check into it. As far as I know we have no former agents now freelancing," she said.

"He said his name was George Wentworth."

Lawson didn't reply, stunned by the name Cain just dropped on her.

"You there?" Cain asked.

"Yeah. Yeah, I'm here," Lawson stuttered, trying not to sound shocked.

"You seem surprised."

"George Wentworth is dead."

"Unless I was talking to a ghost, he seemed very much alive to me."

"George Wentworth was an alias for an agent named Eric Raines. He died six months ago in a warehouse explosion in Indonesia," she said.

"Can you send me a picture of him? I'll confirm whether that's the guy I saw or not."

"Uh, yeah, I'll send one over. I have pictures of all agents on my tablet. Just gimme a sec to pull it up."

Within a couple of minutes Lawson had pulled up a picture of Raines on her iPad. She looked at his face for a second, mixed emotions running through her. The thought of him being alive briefly made her excited for the possibility, cancelling the sadness she previously felt for his loss. She took a big sigh and e-mailed the picture over to Cain.

"OK. It's sent. Check your email," she said.

Cain grabbed his iPad and sat in a chair. He logged into his e-mail and downloaded the picture Lawson sent. With each percentage of the picture that showed on the screen, starting with the top of Raines' head, Cain could see the resemblance to the man he saw. Lawson eagerly awaited Cain's opinion, sighing and leaning on her desk, with her hand holding her head up.

"That's him," Cain said.

Lawson closed her eyes as soon as the words left Cain's lips. She couldn't believe the man they all thought was dead, that they mourned, was actually still alive.

"You're sure that's him?" Lawson asked.

"No doubt about it. That's the guy I saw. Exact same appearance except he's got a goatee now."

"I can't believe it."

"Well, better sink in soon. Because he's alive."

9

Cain's last day spent in Honduras turned up no new leads. He actually tried to soak up some of the country's culture and sampled some of their food, checking out some of their establishments. He contacted Ruiz to see if he could find out anything else on Contreras, like what he was trying to get into. Ruiz came up empty though. All leads died along with Contreras. After he was satisfied there was no further information to be had, Cain flew back to New York.

The entire plane ride home he thought about what Raines told him about not trusting what he was told. He thought about every detail that transpired from the moment he woke up in that army hospital bed until that very second on the plane. Cain closed his eyes as he relived everything. After a few minutes, he stopped thinking and just tried to relax. Relaxing didn't last long as more visions clogged his mind. He tilted his head as if he was trying to get a better view of what he was seeing. The woman who previously appeared was not there this time. On this occasion, it was a little boy. He must've been about four or five years old. He was smiling and laughing as he was playing on a swing set. The boy alternated between the swing and going down the sliding board. The captain's voice came over the intercom detailing the trip, breaking Cain's concentration on the boy. He opened his eyes, and the boy was gone. He closed his eyes again, but the vision was gone for good. He turned his head, looked out the window, and let his mind wander as they flew through the clouds.

A few hours later they landed at JFK airport in New York. Cain's plan was to grab his bag and then take a cab home. He strolled through the airport to the luggage area, where he spotted his bag. He grabbed it, then turned around and noticed Shelly Lawson standing about fifty feet away from him. Cain had told her what flight he was taking home so the agency would be aware of it though Lawson didn't tell him she'd be there waiting for him. He was a little surprised to see her there. He walked over to her, wondering what she wanted.

"Something wrong?" Cain asked.

"No, why?"

"I'm just surprised to see you. What are you doing here?"

"I just thought we should talk about some things," she said.

"Such as?"

"About what happened in Honduras."

"Already told you."

"I need more."

"Don't have anything else to tell you."

"Let's go to my place so we can talk," Lawson said.

Cain stopped walking, surprised at Lawson's request. A quizzical look overtook him, wondering what she was up to. Something didn't seem right. If she really wanted to talk about Honduras, he was curious as to why they weren't going to the Center instead.

"What's this really all about?" Cain asked.

Lawson paused before answering. "I'll tell you when we get there."

"Is this an official request?"

"No. Just as a favor to me," she said.

Cain agreed to her request and continued walking with Lawson on the way to her car, still unsure what she wanted. There was something different about her, though he couldn't place exactly what it was. Maybe it was the determination exuding from her that indicated the seriousness of whatever matter she wanted to discuss.

They arrived at her house an hour after leaving the airport. She lived in a gated community, and judging by the looks of the houses, all the residents seemed to be doing well financially.

"Nice area," Cain said. "Anything up for sale? Maybe I'll move in."

"Not likely. There hasn't been a house for sale here since I moved in over two years ago and that was only because the previous owner passed away."

They went inside and she told Cain to have a seat on the couch while she went into the kitchen. She came back out a minute later, a bottle of soda and water in each hand. She offered Cain his pick of drinks. He grabbed the water, looking it over.

"It's not poisoned if that's what you're looking for," Lawson said, half kidding.

"Just checking," Cain smiled. "Wentworth... Raines, said to not trust anyone. I kinda believed him on it."

"What did he mean by that? Who was he talking about?"

"I don't know. He didn't elaborate."

"What else did he say?"

"Well, he did speak highly of you. He said how good you were and I was in good hands with you. He also said you were the most difficult part of leaving?"

Lawson's eyes started tearing up upon hearing how Raines spoke of her. She missed him since he'd been gone.

"He actually said he left?"

"That's what he said. Why all the questions about him?" Cain asked.

"Like I said, he was supposed to have died six months ago."

"It goes deeper than that, doesn't it?"

"In what way?" Lawson asked.

"Your eyes are tearing up, you seem emotionally involved, and we're here instead of at the Center. You had something personal with him, didn't you?"

Lawson choked back a few tears before answering. "Yes. We were lovers," she admitted. "Although we broke up about a week before he... a week before he died."

"I had a feeling."

"All this time I thought he was dead. I took a leave of absence for two months after his death because it hurt to go to the office knowing I would never see him again. And now he appears, seemingly alive, and if it weren't for you seeing him I still would think he's dead."

"I can see how that'd be upsetting," Cain said. "Seems

pretty unusual. You break up, he dies a week later, six months later he shows up. Sounds like something he had planned in advance."

"But, but why? Why would he do that? What would he gain?" Lawson asked incredulously.

"I think it's pretty obvious. He wanted out. For some reason, he didn't think he could do that any other way. Which means he didn't trust that they'd let him out on his own. So, he cooked up a plan to make it happen."

"I just... I just don't know what to think. If he were alive, why wouldn't he contact me to let me know?"

Cain thought for a few moments, not sure if he should say what he was thinking. He finally relented. "Maybe your feelings for him were stronger than his feelings for you."

"I guess that's possible, isn't it?" she responded, hoping that wasn't the case.

"Or, maybe it's because of the trust thing he was talking about," Cain said. "Maybe something was going on when he died and he wanted to stay that way, not trusting anyone else to keep that secret. Or maybe he was afraid if he contacted you then he'd be found out or that he'd put you in danger. It's tough to know a man's reasons for something unless you're in his shoes."

"This is his file," Lawson said, bringing up his info on her iPad.

Cain carefully looked at each page on the screen. There was personal information, as well as documentation on every mission Raines had ever been on, who some of his known contacts were, as well as the case file on his final mission. Cain reread the information a few times to pick up anything he might've missed the first time around.

"Not a whole lot of information on the Indonesia mission," Cain said.

"That's 'cause we didn't know much about it. He contacted me a day before that and said he was meeting one of his contacts in a warehouse."

"And you don't know who that was?"

"He never said, and we never found out. There were two bodies found, badly burned, neither recognizable."

"How'd they identify him?"

"Dental records," Lawson replied.

"What does Sanders think?"

Lawson hesitated before answering, not really sure how to reply.

"You didn't tell him yet?" Cain inferred.

"Not exactly."

"Why not? What are you waiting for?"

"I don't know. I guess I'm waiting for the right time," she said.

"Don't you trust him?"

"Yeah, I guess," Lawson said. "I mean, I don't know. The whole organization is based on lies and secrecy, and lies based on lies, that it's tough to know what to believe sometimes."

"Wait," Cain said.

"What?" Lawson replied.

"He was in Indonesia before, about a year ago," he said, looking at his missions.

"Yes. He was following up on something about some arms dealer. Turned out to be nothing."

"Says he met with someone named Aditya Gutawa."

"We contacted him after Eric died to see if he knew anything about it. He said he didn't know and hadn't seen Eric since last year."

"And you believed him?"

"Why would he lie?"

"If Raines went to Gutawa and asked for his help, don't you think he'd help the man he worked with, developed a relationship with, help him disappear if that's what he wanted… or a government agency he probably doesn't care shit about."

"But we asked him—," Lawson started to say before being interrupted.

"But you're the government agency. He's not gonna tell you."

"You're right."

"You also need to accept another possibility," Cain said.

"Which is what?"

"That he's not the same man you once knew. The man you knew and loved, maybe he was a good man, maybe he had good intentions, I don't know. But you have to face that he might not be that man anymore. He dropped off the planet for a reason. And those reasons might not be all that pleasant once you find them."

"I know," she said solemnly, nodding.

Lawson leaned back on her sofa, letting Cain's words sink in. She knew he was right but didn't want to believe that Raines turned his back on her. Cain finished looking at Raines' file and turned off the computer, handing it back to Lawson.

"We need answers," Lawson said.

"We?"

"I mean the agency. We need to know what happened to him."

"You mean you need answers," Cain said.

"You're right. I do. But we also need to know if there's something bigger at work here. Not only that, but he knows everything we do. He knows how we think and act. If he has his own agenda now that doesn't mesh with ours, then he could put all our agents at risk. We need to find out what he's up to now."

"And how do you propose to do that?"

"How would you feel about going to Indonesia?" she asked.

Cain looked at her like she was crazy. He wasn't sure he bought what she was saying about the agency needing to find Raines as much as it was driving her insane that she didn't know what happened to him. Cain and Lawson talked for another hour about the situation and about how they'd present it to Sanders. Lawson offered to let Cain stay the night if he wanted, sleeping on the couch, but he wanted to get back to his place and relax. She drove him home, getting him to his apartment about seven o'clock. Lawson told Cain she'd let him know what Sanders said if she asked him about Indonesia.

He walked into his apartment, looking around for Heather, and shouting her name. He walked around from room to room, seeing how the place looked. The bed was made, and the rooms were clean, almost like she hadn't even been there. He walked over to the desk and noticed the PC was on. He awakened it from sleep mode and looked at the website that popped up. A couple tabs were on there, both job related sites. Cain then walked into the kitchen and noticed a couple plates in the sink. He looked in the refrigerator to see what there was to eat and pulled out some lunch meat, making himself a turkey sandwich. He sat down on the couch to eat and put the TV on, flipping channels until he came across a Yankees game. With almost every pitch thrown he wondered where Heather was. He assumed she would've been there when he got home. He hoped she didn't go back to her apartment or meet up with someone. An hour passed by when he heard some rattling just outside the door. It sounded like someone was fumbling with keys. Cain went to the kitchen drawer and opened it, putting his hand on the handle of his Glock, just in case it was an unwanted visitor. The door handle jiggled before opening, Heather walking in, a couple of bags in each hand. Cain took his hand off the gun and closed the drawer. She stopped and almost screamed when she saw Cain standing there, holding her hand over her heart and sighing like she almost had a heart attack.

"You almost scared me," she said.

"Almost?"

Heather continued walking into the living room, putting the bags down on the table.

"OK. Maybe a little bit. What are you doing here?"

"Umm, I'm pretty sure I live here," Cain said sarcastically.

"Obviously. I mean, I didn't expect you back so late at night."

"Well, I got back a few hours ago. I had to go over a few things first about Honduras."

"Oh. Was it a good trip?" Heather asked, not quite knowing how to ask about it.

"Had its good moments and bad."

"Oh. Anything you wanna talk about?"

"No," he responded, shaking his head. "Did you have fun while I was gone?"

"Oh yeah. Loads and loads."

"What'd you do?"

"Spent most of the time job hunting. When I got bored with that fun stuff, I did other exciting things, you know, like eating and sleeping."

"Sounds like a great time," Cain said.

"Oh. It was. It was."

"Whatcha got in those bags?"

"Oh, I went shopping," she said and smiled. "I've got two interviews tomorrow, so I wanted to get some new outfits for them."

"Good for you. What jobs are they?"

"One is for an entry level marketing position. And the other is for a payroll specialist at a payroll company."

"Nice. I hope you get one of them."

"Yeah, me too."

"I'm sure you'll do great."

"I don't know. I'm a little nervous."

"Just go in there prepared and show your stuff," he said.

"Well, I'm used to showing my stuff, but I'm not sure that's what they have in mind," she kidded.

Cain laughed, then reassured her that she'd be fine. Heather wanted to try the outfits on and asked him if he could tell her how she looked in them. In truth, she'd already tried them on in the store before she bought them and knew how they looked, but she wanted to get his opinion on them. Plus, she hoped it'd get Cain more interested in her. She went into the bedroom and changed into a blue skirt outfit that wasn't as revealing as most of the things in her wardrobe. After Cain gave her good reviews she then changed into a tighter fitting suit outfit, complete with black high heels. Cain looked her up and down, pleased with the view, and told her how good she looked.

"If you interview as good as you look, then you'll get the job hands-down," Cain said.

"Thanks," she replied, smiling ear to ear.

They talked a little more about the jobs, Cain helping her prepare for the interviews by asking her some questions. She knew the basics about each company and wrote down questions and some possible answers to them.

"Still nervous?" Cain asked.

"Yeah, but excited too. I feel like this is the beginning of a new chapter in my life. I feel good about moving on. But it's always scary when something new comes along."

"Yeah. You'll do great though," he said, putting his arm around her.

Heather hoped he'd take it further than that brief hug but was disappointed when he didn't make any other moves.

"Well, I guess I should get to bed. The first interview is at nine."

"When's the second one?" Cain asked.

"Noon."

"Maybe when you're done we could meet somewhere for lunch if you want?"

"Yeah, I'd like that."

They decided on a restaurant and agreed to meet at one, figuring Heather would be done with her interview.

She then walked into the bedroom and brought out a pillow, placing it on the couch.

"What're you doing?" Cain asked.

"Going to bed."

"No, no, no. Get back in there," he said, pointing to the bedroom.

"What? I'm not sleeping in your bed."

At least not by herself, she thought. She wouldn't have minded sleeping in there with him, but she didn't want to take it on her own.

"Where'd you sleep while I was gone?"

"In your bed," she replied.

"Then there you go."

"But you're back now and I'm not gonna take your bed away from you."

"Heather, I was in the military, I'm used to not sleeping in beds. I could sleep in the bathtub if I had to."

Heather tried resisting one more time, but Cain wouldn't let her say no.

"Besides, you have a big day tomorrow, you need to get a good, comfortable sleep. You can't be scrunched up on the couch all night," he said. "Take the bed. Get a good night's sleep."

She finally relented, knowing she wasn't going to win the fight. She really wanted to give him a kiss and hug goodnight but wanted to give him space since he obviously was taking things slow.

In the middle of the night Cain started tossing and turning in his sleep while he was dreaming. He saw himself back in the army, in an old, abandoned building. It appeared that he was in some desolate town, very sunny with high winds, dust and dirt kicking up and swirling everywhere. He was in an upstairs window with a sniper rifle waiting for his victim to walk into his crosshairs. A man in a suit walked into his path but for some reason his face was blurry. He couldn't make out who the man was. The man stuck out, his suit seeming like odd attire for the kind of place they were in. Cain lined the man up for an easy shot, slowly pulling the trigger on his rifle. A shot rang out. The bullet moved at a snail's pace. Cain could see it traveling through the air, almost like a movie slowing the frame down. Once the bullet got close to its intended target it sped up like it was in fast forward, hitting the man square in the forehead, the bullet lodging in his head. The man instantly dropped to his knees before falling onto the ground, face down. Like he was transported, Cain was suddenly standing over the man's dead body. He knelt down to see who the man was and turned him over. It was him. He shot himself in the head. Cain suddenly woke up startled, screaming, almost jumping off the couch. He sat there, elbows on his knees, head down, sweat pouring off his body. Heather woke up once she heard Cain scream and stood in the doorway to the living room where she saw him sitting there. He was still sweating and heavily sighing. She ran to the couch and sat next to him, putting her arms around him, and then put his head on her shoulder as she stroked his head to relax him.

"It's OK," she whispered.

She was concerned because he was still breathing heavily and he was sweating like he just spent three hours at the gym. She thought of calling the doctor but decided to give him a few more minutes to calm down. He didn't seem like he was in pain, just startled.

"Are you OK?"

"Yeah," he replied.

"What happened?"

"I just had a dream."

"What was it about?" she asked, still clutching on to him.

"I was back in the military. A sniper," he told her, his breathing starting to slow. "And I shot someone in the head and killed him."

"It was just a dream."

"No. I went to check on him and when I turned him over and saw who it was... it was me. I killed myself."

"Shh. It's OK," she said.

Heather continued holding him until he stopped sweating, and his breathing returned to normal. About twenty minutes later Cain fell back asleep, in her arms, as she leaned back on the sofa. So much for getting a good night's sleep in bed, she thought to herself. She really didn't mind though as holding him was exactly what she was craving. If she lost an hour or so of sleep it wasn't a big deal. She'd rather have made sure he was OK first. She hoped he didn't have any more episodes for the night, not worrying about her sleep, but genuinely concerned for his well-being. She fell asleep a short time later, content to still be holding him.

Cain woke up a few hours later, free from any further dreams, and looked toward the light shining in through the window. He glanced at the clock which just turned seven. He picked his head up off Heather's shoulder and looked at her. She looked so peaceful lying there. She really was a beautiful woman, he thought. Cain was appreciative of her looking after him and taking care of him, especially after his latest episode. The alarm clock in the bedroom went off, Cain going in to stop it, then waking Heather up. She was one of those naturally beautiful women who looked great with no makeup or even with her hair messed up.

"Hey," she said. "How you feeling?"

"I'm OK."

"Good. You scared me a little last night."

"I scared myself," Cain said. "Thank you, though, for sitting with me and all. I appreciate it."

"You're welcome. That's what friends are for, right?"

"I heard the alarm go off, so I figured you wanted to get up now."

"Oh, yeah. Thanks. I have to shower. I probably look like crap," she said, running her hand through her hair.

"I don't think it's possible for you to look anything other than beautiful," he said.

A huge smile came over Heather's face, the compliment making her blush.

"Why are you blushing?" Cain asked.

"I dunno," she said, still smiling, looking away. "I'm used to fake compliments. You know, people who say something just because they think it'll get them somewhere."

"Maybe that's what I'm doing."

"No, it's not. I can tell. You say things because you mean them. It's genuine coming from you. That's a refreshing change."

Heather went in to take a shower, hoping someone would join her, though she knew it wouldn't happen. She was right, as Cain started making breakfast. He wanted to show her another sign of appreciation for what she'd done for him. It was nothing special, just pancakes, but he hoped she'd like it. He put the food on the table as she got out of the shower and changed. Once she came out, she saw breakfast waiting on the table for her.

"Aww. You're so sweet," she remarked, genuinely touched.

"Nothing fancy, but at least it's not burnt."

"No, it's great. Thank you," she said, kissing him on the cheek.

"Just my way of saying thank you for last night, and before," he said.

"Well, it's not necessary, but it's really nice of you."

They sat down and ate, talking some more about the interviews she was about to go on. Once they were done she finished getting ready and left by eight, wanting to get there in plenty of time. Cain passed the time by reading the news on the internet.

10

Specter Project Center—Ed Sanders was walking into his office when his secretary rushed in behind him before he even had a chance to sit down.

"Sir, there was someone looking at agents' files last night," his secretary said.

"Whose?"

"Eric Raines."

"Who was looking at it?"

"Shelly Lawson," she replied, looking at her paper, handing it to him.

Sanders sighed, disappointment covering his face, as he wondered what exactly she was looking for.

"Is Shelly in her office?" Sanders asked.

"I believe she is," his secretary said. "I'll double check for you, sir."

"Please do. If she is, will you please ask her to come in here?"

"I will."

"Thank you."

The secretary went to Lawson's office to find her. Lawson was just getting off the phone as her visitor walked in.

"Mr. Sanders would like to see you."

"OK. I'll be right there."

As Lawson walked to Sanders office, she wondered what he wanted to talk about. She thought about whether she should tell him about Cain finding Raines in Honduras, whether she should just keep it to herself for a while, or whether she should send Cain to Indonesia without telling Sanders. If she did and Sanders eventually found out she was withholding information from him, it could jeopardize her standing. She always tried to stay above board with everything.

Lawson walked into Sanders office, his eyes focused directly on her. She could tell he knew something. She could just see it in his face.

"Shelly, I was reading your report on Cain's adventure in Honduras," Sanders said.

"It's a little incomplete," she replied. "I have to revise some of it."

"Oh? I was under the impression this was all of it."

A slight hesitation engulfed her before she finally relented on telling her secret. She knew it was better to just come out with it like she was volunteering the information rather than have him dig for it, knowing it'd come out, anyway.

"I had to do some checking on something Cain told me," Lawson said.

"Which was?"

"Cain said the man who killed Contreras identified himself as George Wentworth."

"The alias of Eric Raines," Sanders said. "I noticed you looked into his file last night. You know those files aren't for general viewing."

"I pulled up his file and had Cain look at his picture to see if it was the same man he saw."

"And?" Sanders asked, seemingly convinced that it was a plausible explanation.

"It was," she said.

"And you believe it?"

"Cain said there's no doubt that's the man he saw in Honduras. Plus, he used one of his aliases so I tend to believe that he is in fact alive."

"Well, I don't even know what to say to that," Sanders puffed, stroking his chin in thought, trying to keep his composure.

"I believe we should send someone to Indonesia," Lawson said.

"You do realize we had confirmation of his death, do you not?"

"I do, sir."

"Then what makes you think by sending someone to Indonesia six months later, that we'll find out anything different?"

"I would like to send someone there to talk to one of his contacts he made over a year ago, a man named Aditya Gutawa."

"Did we not talk to him before?"

"Only briefly. There was no reason to question him further at the time. We thought Raines was dead," Lawson said. "Now that we know he's alive..."

"And you think Gutawa knows something?"

"I would like to find out."

"What are your reasons for this?" Sanders asked.

"To find out why he was presumed dead and six months later is found alive."

"Is that it? Or are your reasons more... personal?"

"I will admit I do have personal feelings," Lawson said. "But this goes beyond that. As much as I hate to admit it, we need to find out what happened and why. The fact that he shows up six months later in Honduras, and killing one of our targets, suggests he didn't just wanna drop off the map. He's still involved in some capacity and we need to find out where he stands in the game. If he's now playing on the other side, he could possibly compromise our entire operation."

"Who do you propose sending?"

"I'd like to send Cain," she said.

"Why him?"

"My other agents are deployed elsewhere, and I'd rather not pull them off. Plus, I believe Cain can get the information we need."

"You have a lot of faith in him."

"I do. He also is the reason we know Raines is alive."

"That's irrelevant," Sanders said.

"I know. I agree, but he's also a newer agent who has no opinion of him from before and has no ties to him which will not cloud his judgment on the situation."

"That I will agree with."

Lawson waited silently as Sanders sat there thinking about the best course of action. He agreed on what she was proposing.

"If you want Cain, you got him," he said. "When do you want to send him?"

"Within the next two or three days if possible."

"Get it done."

Lawson left the office to get to work on Cain's excursion. She needed to quickly get his flight together and the logistics of his stay. She also put out some feelers to people she knew to get the whereabouts on Gutawa. She didn't want to call Cain until she got more specifics on everything. Once noon came around, she started to get a better idea of what was happening. She was waiting for one more person to call her back on where Gutawa was.

Cain had just taken a seat at the restaurant he was meeting Heather at, waiting for her. The restaurant had outdoor seating, which considering the nice day that it was, Cain felt Heather would like. It was five minutes to one, so he was sure she would be there soon. He'd gotten a text from her fifteen minutes before that saying she was done with her interview and was on her way. He ordered drinks for the two of them while he waited. Just as he looked at the time on his phone again, it started ringing. Once he saw it was Lawson, he knew something was up.

"What's going on?" Cain asked.

"You're going to Indonesia," Lawson replied.

"When?"

"Tomorrow morning."

"Not much time to prepare."

"How much time do you need?" Lawson asked.

"None. It's good."

"Your flight leaves at 7:20am."

"Couldn't leave any earlier than that, huh?" Cain joked.

"It's a long flight."

"How long?"

"Better take some DVDs," she joked.

"Great."

"You'll fly to Heathrow Airport in Great Britain. From there you'll fly to Singapore and then to Jakarta, Indonesia, where you'll arrive at 6:05pm Saturday."

"Twenty-three hours?"

"That's the quickest they got."

"Fantastic."

"What are you doing right now?"

"About to have lunch," Cain said as he spotted Heather walking into the restaurant.

"Well, when you're done, come in. Sanders wants to have a word with you."

"I will do that."

Cain hung up just as Heather sat down. She looked like she was in a good mood, indicating the interviews went well.

"Who were you talking to?" she asked.

"Just business. How'd your interviews go?" he asked, brushing the question aside.

"I think they went really well. Preparing for them was the big thing."

"When are they gonna let you know?"

"Well, they both said they have other people to talk to, so it could be about a week or so."

"You'll get one of them."

"I hope so. Who'd you say you were talking to?" she asked again, knowing he tried to avoid telling her.

"Just someone from the office."

"You're just not gonna tell me anything, are you?"

Just as he was about to reply the waiter came over to take their order. They took turns ordering and Cain tried to switch the subject to something else, which Heather was not having any part of. It wasn't so much that she wanted to know the person who was calling more so than just wanting to be a bigger part of Cain's life and hoping that he'd eventually start confiding in her.

"Why won't you tell me anything?"

"Why do you wanna know?" Cain asked.

"I don't know, we're friends, and I'm living in your apartment right now. What you do kind of affects me."

"Listen, you know I can't tell you what I do."

"I didn't ask that. All I asked was who called. You can't tell me that?"

"It was Michelle," Cain finally said. "You remember her, right?"

"Oh yes. She doesn't like me too much. I guess I can't say I blame her."

"Maybe you two just got off on the wrong foot."

"I don't think there'll ever be a right foot with her. She called with good news I hope?"

"I have to go somewhere," Cain said.

"Where? Are you able to say?"

"Indonesia?"

"Indonesia? Where's that?" Heather asked.

"Southeast Asia."

"Oh. Important I guess?"

"I suppose so."

"When do you leave?"

"Tomorrow morning," Cain said.

"Oh," Heather said, dejected.

"What's wrong?"

"Well, you just got back from a trip. I just thought you'd be here for a while. Was looking forward to that hockey game," she said, trying to make it not sound like she was going to miss him.

"Yeah, well, I guess we'll have to try for a game once I get back. You'll look after the place while I'm gone?"

"Of course. How long will you be?"

"I don't know. Probably a few days."

Heather was so disappointed that Cain was leaving again, although she tried not to outwardly show it. She wanted to spend some time with him, whether it was going out somewhere, or just staying in the apartment, talking and hanging out. She was so upset about him leaving that she really didn't enjoy the idea of having lunch together. The fact Cain told her he was leaving the next morning made it more difficult for her to accept since he just got back. She knew it'd be tough for their relationship to grow to where she wanted it to go if he was always going away somewhere.

After having lunch, Heather went back to the apartment, while Cain went to the Center to talk to Sanders and get the rest of the mission from Lawson. He was directed to go to Sanders' office first. Sanders got off the phone a minute after Cain walked in.

"I'm gonna keep this brief," Sanders said. "First, good job in Honduras, good work."

"Thanks."

"I just wanna make sure we're clear about Indonesia. You're there to get information."

"Yeah."

"By any means necessary," he told him. "I don't care how you get the information we need. Just get it."

"I understand," Cain replied.

"Good. Do what you have to do. Shelly's waiting for you in her office."

Cain went straight to Lawson's office, who'd been waiting for him. He sat down in the chair in front of her desk as she got out the paperwork.

"Here's your itinerary," she said.

"Such a long flight," Cain said.

"Well, that's why you're gonna have company."

"What?"

"You're getting a partner for this mission."

"Why? It's a pretty simple objective," he said.

"Well, just in case there are any unexpected surprises."

"Who is it?"

"They'll meet you at the airport."

Lawson talked about the culture of Indonesia, letting Cain know what to expect. The country consisted of over 17,000 islands and was the largest archipelago in the world. They also had the fourth largest population in the world, with over 85% of its inhabitants Muslim, also the largest in the world. They'd be flying into Jakarta, the capital and largest city. Robbery, theft, and pick-pocketing was common there, though most crime was non-violent and guns were rare. Indonesia was one of the most corrupt countries in the world as officials often asked for bribes to supplement their salaries. Though they had a corrupt legal system, they did deal with drug usage harshly. There's "Death To Drug Traffickers" signs at airports, and the death penalty was mandatory for those convicted of trafficking, manufacturing, importing, or exporting, and a person could be charged with such if drugs were found in their possession even if they weren't aware of it. Even though the penalties were harsh, drugs were common, especially cocaine, ecstasy, and crystal methamphetamine.

"So, where do I look for Gutawa?" Cain asked.

"Here," Lawson replied, handing him a paper with an address on it.

"What's this?"

"His address."

"You got his address?"

"Took some doing, and talking to a few people, but I tracked him down."

"Wow. You are good," Cain said, gushing.

"I know," she replied, and smiled.

Cain went back to his apartment to pack his bags once they finished going over their business in the office. Heather was on the computer looking up more jobs.

"Still going at it?" Cain asked.

"Well, just in case those other two don't pan out, I figured I should keep applying for other jobs."

"Good idea."

"How was your meeting?" she asked.

"Fine."

"When's your flight?"

"Early. I'll be gone by the time you wake up," he said.

"Oh. Don't know when you'll be back?"

"Shouldn't be long. Can't say exactly though. Takes a day just to fly there. So, it'll be two days just being in the air."

JFK airport—Cain was sitting in the terminal, waiting for his partner to arrive, though he didn't know how he'd know the guy since they didn't tell him who was going with him. About half an hour before they needed to board Cain looked around and noticed Lawson walking toward him. He noticed she was carrying a bag with her.

"Hey," she said.

"Hey. Going somewhere?"

"I did say someone was going with you."

"I assumed it was another agent," Cain said.

"I thought you might have a problem if I told you it was me."

"Does Sanders know about this?"

"I told him. He was fine with it."

"Why am I even going?" Cain asked.

"I'm an information girl. I know how to get it once I know what I'm looking for. I'm not trained in combat. In case something goes down, you're the muscle," she kidded.

"Reassuring."

11

Jakarta, Indonesia—Once Cain and Lawson touched down, they traveled using an AC minibus. It was nighttime and was the most effective and easiest way of travel. Renting a car was dangerous in Indonesia, as they usually had very bad driving habits. They'd often drive on the shoulder of the road, making lane changes and passing other cars dangerously. They also often ignored traffic lights. Using the minibus was more expensive, but it was the safest way of driving. They immediately went to the address they had for Gutawa. He had a pretty nice looking two-story house that indicated he had some wealth. There was often a very stark contrast in Indonesia; you could see who was wealthy standing right next to those who were in extreme poverty. Lawson knocked on the door but there was no answer. There were no lights on so it appeared Gutawa was out.

"Come back later?" Lawson asked.

"You can. I ain't coming back later though," Cain said, as he picked the lock of the door.

"I'm not sure this is wise."

"Listen, I'd like to get out of this country as soon as possible. This isn't my idea of a vacation so the sooner we get this over with the better. Besides, how do you know when we come back he'll be here, anyway? We'll wait."

While they were waiting, they looked around for a computer. They weren't positive Gutawa had one, but they searched anyway. They looked through the living room and kitchen, before finally finding a laptop in a table drawer in his bedroom next to his bed. Lawson turned it on and searched through some files to see if there was anything of interest on there but she didn't notice anything important. She then installed tracking software on the machine that would pick up any e-mails that he received and immediately send a copy of them to her without being traced. Gutawa could find the bug they installed if he was looking for it, but it was likely he wouldn't discover it for quite some time. Their wait didn't last long, about an hour. Gutawa walked in the door and turned a light on, seeing Lawson sitting on his couch.

"What you doing here?" Gutawa asked. Most Indonesians spoke English capably.

"I want to talk to you. Come sit down," Lawson said.

"Get out of my house."

"I think you best sit down," Cain said from behind him.

Gutawa complied with their wishes, figuring they had other things on their minds if he did not.

"We're not here to hurt you," Lawson said. "We just want information."

"About what?"

"Eric Raines."

"What about him?"

"We know you were one of his contacts," she said.

"He died over six months ago."

"No, he did not."

Gutawa didn't reply to that, looking at both of his visitors, not seeming very surprised by the revelation.

"Judging by the look on your face, you already knew that," Cain said.

"I know nothing."

"Well, we think you do," Cain added, taking his Glock out of his belt, making sure Gutawa saw it.

"No. We don't need that," Lawson said. "Listen, we know he's alive. We've seen him. You don't have to hide it anymore."

"Why do you want to know where he is?"

"Because we need to know what he plans on doing. Whether he's in trouble and needs our help, or whether he's intending to do bad things. Either way, we need to find him."

Gutawa kept looking at Cain, who clenched the grip of his gun in front of his body. Gutawa seemed quite sure the man would use the gun on him if he chose not to give them the information they were seeking.

"What you want to know?" he asked.

"What happened to him?" Lawson asked.

"He came to me one year ago asking for my help. He said he was in trouble with some people and he needed to disappear."

"Trouble from whom?"

"He said the people he works for were getting close to him and were going to kill him soon."

"What? That's crazy," Lawson said. "Nothing like that was true."

"He come to me and asked if I could help him become a dead man. I say I cannot help in that matter but I know someone who can."

"Who'd you send him to?" Cain asked.

"His name is Guntur. You can find him at Ragunan Zoo. He works there sometimes."

Gutawa gave the pair Guntur's physical description so they could find him. The three of them continued talking about Raines, trying to get an idea of what he was working on.

"Have you heard from Raines in the last six months?" Cain asked.

"I have not," Gutawa answered.

"Do you know what his plans are?"

"No."

Lawson and Cain talked with Gutawa for another hour, trying to extract more information out of him, but they got to the point where he had nothing else to tell them. He seemed to be forthright with them and didn't appear to be holding anything back. He seemed rightfully afraid of the duo that broke into his house and knew they weren't playing games.

"Here's my info," Cain said, writing his number on a piece of paper, and handing it to Gutawa. "You hear from him, you call me."

"I will."

"If I find out he contacts you and you don't let me know, I'll come back and kill you," Cain said bluntly.

"I understand."

The pair left Gutawa's home and went back to their hotel for the night. They were pleased with what they got out of Gutawa. Not only did he divulge the name of the man who helped Raines, they were sure they'd wind up getting something useful from his computer.

"Do you think he'll contact Raines?" Lawson asked.

"I think it's likely he will at some point."

"Why?"

"If he feels loyal enough to him to help him disappear, then it's logical to assume he's likely to contact him at some point to tell him people know he's not dead and that they're looking for him," Cain replied.

"How long do you think it'll take?"

"Few days, maybe a week, maybe more. He'll probably wait until he's reasonably sure we've gone in a different direction."

The Ragunan Zoo didn't open until 8am the following morning so they had some time to wait. The zoo was a world class facility and housed over 500 species of plants and animals from around the world, including the Sumatran tiger and Komodo dragon. Once they got into their room, they discovered they had a bit of a situation.

"There's only one bed," Cain said.

"What?"

"You said it."

"That can't be. I booked..." Lawson started before realizing what happened.

"Yes?"

She grimaced. "When I made the reservations, it was

just you going. Once I changed the plans, I forgot to change the hotel reservations."

"Fantastic," Cain added sarcastically.

"Wait, it's fine. I'll just call down to the desk and get another room."

Lawson called down to the desk and requested another room. As she was speaking, her facial expressions indicated to Cain that she wasn't having much luck. She hung up the phone with an almost painful expression.

"Well? How'd that turn out?" Cain asked, already knowing the answer.

"Umm, not well. It seems they're all booked up for the night."

Cain sighed. "Well, I guess you take the bed and I'll take the floor."

"I'm really sorry."

"It's OK. I've been meaning to sleep on the floor lately. It's a good chance to get my back used to it again."

They both sat down and went on their computers for a little bit, Lawson to do some work on hers, Cain just surfing the internet. After an hour, Lawson put hers away and went to take a shower. After she finished, she came out in just a towel, barely covering her essentials. Cain tried not to pay attention but couldn't help but take a few glances in her direction as she sauntered across the room. She went to her bag on the bed and pulled out a brush, noticing that Cain was periodically glancing over at her. She hadn't been intimate with anyone since Raines broke up with her. It was nice to have someone still looking at her in a lusty manner. Cain, in an effort to get his mind off her, went in to take a shower as well. While he was showering Lawson had thoughts of surprising him in there, but she thought better of it, since it really wouldn't be professional or appropriate. She was attracted to him but she had second thoughts since she got burned the last time she had a relationship with one of her agents. She sat down on the bed and brushed her hair, getting thoughts of him out of her mind. He came out fifteen minutes later, just a towel covering his waist, and meandered over to the bed. His bag was next to Lawson's. She got up to give Cain some room, brushing up against him, accidentally knocking his towel off him. They looked at each other, both unsure that they should go any further.

"Oh, what the hell," Lawson said, leaning in to kiss him.

Cain returned her kiss and unwrapped Lawson from her towel. He picked her up and laid her on the bed. Though they both knew they shouldn't be doing it, neither was interested in stopping.

The following morning the two of them got dressed and headed to the zoo. Although neither was ashamed or embarrassed by what happened the night before, it was a bit uncomfortable between them.

"About last night," Lawson said. "It was great."

"But?"

"But we probably should leave it at that. It's not a good idea for either one of us to get involved."

"I agree," Cain said.

"Especially after what's happened with Raines, I just don't know if I can go through all that again."

"It's OK. Really. There's nothing wrong with leaving things as they are. We had a fun night. I'm OK with that."

"But it was great, wasn't it?" Lawson asked, smiling.

"Yeah."

They arrived at the zoo and went their separate ways, walking around trying to spot Guntur. If either of them spotted him they'd call the other to their location. They spent about five hours between walking and sitting, waiting to line Guntur up in their sights, before they finally got an eye on him. Cain was sitting by the Komodo dragon exhibit when he spotted him walking around, picking up litter, emptying trash cans. He called Lawson to let her know.

"I've got him," Cain said.

"Where?"

"Come to the Komodo dragon exhibit."

"On my way."

To prevent him from leaving the area before Lawson got there, Cain started to approach their target.

"Guntur," Cain said.

Guntur looked a little worried that the American knew his name. That could only mean bad news. He looked around like he was about to run.

"Let's sit down for a minute," Cain said, opening his jacket to show his gun.

Cain hoped that letting Guntur see his weapon would make him think twice about taking off.

"Now, about sitting down," Cain said once more.

Guntur nodded, agreeing to Cain's request. Cain grabbed hold of his arm to make sure he didn't take off on him. They sat down on the bench as they waited for Lawson to appear.

"First thing is I'm not gonna hurt you," Cain said. "All I want is information. You take off on me or feed me a bunch of crap and I'm gonna change my mind.

Understood?"

"Yes."

Lawson quickly arrived, almost out of breath from scurrying over.

"How do you know me?" Guntur asked.

"Doesn't matter. We only want you to piece some things together for us," Cain said.

"What can I tell you?" Guntur asked the pair.

"Eric Raines, what happened to him?"

"He died six months ago."

"What'd I tell you?" Cain replied, shoving the gun in his side.

"What about him?" Guntur relented.

"We know you helped him fake his death," Lawson said. "How?"

Guntur seemed surprised his companions were asking about Raines, or even knew about him faking his death. Cain could see Guntur still had reservations about talking so he pushed the gun further into his side, causing the slightest bit of pain.

"I'm not telling you again," Cain said sternly.

"He was sent to me about faking his death."

"I already know that."

Guntur heavily sighed and resigned himself to telling the pair the information they were seeking. "We came up with blowing up a warehouse with him inside."

"How'd you get around verifying the body?" Lawson asked.

"You must understand, the Indonesian government is very corrupt. For a few extra dollars, you can find someone willing to switch records or create documents to say anything."

"What exactly did he need you for?"

"He came to me with what he wanted. I know the proper people who can make that happen. I am mostly a middle man."

"For a fee," Cain said.

"Of course."

"I'm assuming you get paid well for that sort of thing."

"Yes."

"Then what are you doing working here?" Cain asked.

"It's good cover. Plus, if I ever need to do business, I can blend in. Plenty of people walking around here. Easy to get lost in the crowd," Guntur explained.

"Did Raines tell you why he wanted to fake his death?" Lawson asked.

"No. Man who wants to do that has his own reasons. Not for me to know. Or to ask."

"Do you know where he was going after leaving here?" Lawson pressed.

"No."

"Is there anything else you can tell us about him? Anybody else he may have talked to while he was here?" Cain asked.

"No. As far as I know it was just me. I got the documents for him and off he went. What he did after me I couldn't say."

"OK." Cain sighed in frustration.

"Wait, one other thing," Guntur said. "When I let him know everything was taken care of he received a phone call in my presence."

"What'd he say?"

"I don't know. It was in a language I cannot understand."

"How long did it last?"

"Only few minutes. He kept saying nyet, nyet. He seemed a little angry after he was done though."

"Russian," Cain said to Lawson.

"Kurylenko," Lawson returned.

"They're working together."

Cain reached into his pocket and handed Guntur a 2,000 rupiah note. A big grin surfaced on Guntur's face, appreciative of the money. Cain also gave him his phone number, and received Guntur's as well, in case he ever had any information for him.

"You learn anything else, you call me," Cain said.

"You work for U.S. government?" Guntur asked.

"Maybe."

"I ever hear anything else about different things, maybe I call you about that too?"

"I don't wanna hear about old ladies getting hit in the street. But if it's big, you let me know," Cain said.

"And maybe I get more of these?" Guntur asked, holding the rupiah note up.

"Depends how good the information is."

He smiled. "Guntur only has good information."

"Well, you take care of yourself."

Cain and Lawson walked around the zoo for a little bit, looking at the animals, while also discussing Raines. They tried to figure out what his plans were or where he might be but didn't have much luck coming up with any answers. After the zoo, they went back to their hotel to continue brainstorming, Lawson trying to dig up anything she could on her computer. After still not coming up with anything, she called Sanders to let him know of their findings. Although finding out he was probably in league with Kurylenko was a good start, she wasn't prepared to hear the news that Sanders had for her.

"Well, we've just received some information here about Raines," Sanders said.

"Oh? What's that?" Lawson asked, surprised.

"We got word about eight or nine hours ago that one of our agents was killed in Mexico meeting with an informant."

"Oh my God. Who was it?" she asked, concerned.

"Danson. Both he and the informant were eliminated."

"Do we know who did it?"

"Not at first," Sanders said. "But we were able to get our hands on some surveillance footage of the building next to where they were located. Came in about two hours ago. It showed a man leaving that building minutes after the two of them were killed."

"Have we identified who the man is yet?"

"We have," Sanders replied. "It was Eric Raines."

Lawson was stunned to hear that Raines had killed one of their agents, someone who used to be on the same side as him. She didn't know what to say upon hearing the news.

"You there, Shelly?"

"Yes. I'm here. Are we positive it's him?" she asked, hoping it was a mistake.

"It is confirmed. The facial recognition software positively ID'd him. There's no doubt it's him."

"So, what's our next step?"

"His picture and file has been sent to every field agent, handler, executive, and support staff to get familiar with him. I've ordered a KOS on him. No questions asked," Sanders said.

"I see."

"I'm sorry, Shelly. I know it's difficult for you but we have no choice now that he's killed one of our agents. We now know which side he's on and it isn't ours."

"I know."

"Get back to New York as soon as you can."

"Our flight's leaving tomorrow," Lawson said.

As soon as Lawson got off the phone, Cain could see she was troubled by something. She was trying very hard not to break down and cry, though eventually a tear ran down her cheek. She quickly wiped it away, not wanting Cain to see it.

"What's wrong?" Cain asked.

"One of our agents was killed in Mexico."

"Who was it?"

"He said they have video of Raines leaving the building minutes after our agent was killed," she struggled to say.

"I'm sorry."

"Me too," Lawson said, managing to let a fake smile through.

"What's the next move?"

"We'll have to go back to New York and see. But in the meantime, Sanders has issued a KOS on Raines."

"KOS? What's that?" Cain asked.

"Kill on sight. It's very rare for that to be issued. It's only ordered for top priority cases where the other options are limited or exhausted. They don't like to issue it because it's dangerous for the field agents. If they run into a KOS target, then they're supposed to kill that target no matter where they are, whether it's in public or not. It could be in the middle of a crowded street. It exposes the agent as well as possibly compromising them along with the mission they were on. There's only been two other times the order's been issued since I've been working there."

"He's now a threat."

"You know, it was only a month or so ago where I stopped thinking about him every day and felt like I was actually starting to move on. And now this, just brings the hurt back even more," she said.

"It's gonna hurt again once someone finally kills him," Cain said. "And it will come to that."

"I know," she said sorrowfully.

"How did you break up?" Cain asked, trying to think of a way to tie everything together.

"Huh? Why does it matter?"

"Just curious."

"He broke up with me a week before he supposedly died. He said he felt like he had too much going on and just needed a break for a while."

Cain sat back in his chair, just thinking about Raines. He tried to put himself in Raines' shoes to get an idea of what he would do if he did the same thing. Cain shot a weird look over to Lawson that worried her.

"What?" she asked.

"Just thinking," he said, trying to think of the best way to phrase his thoughts.

"You got something?"

"I'm not sure."

"Well, just say it."

"He broke up with you a week before he died," Cain said.

"Yeah?"

"Well, we know he was planning this for at least six months to a year before that."

"What are you getting at?"

"That maybe he was using you to get information," Cain said.

"Information about what?"

"Where agents were located, types of missions being worked on, anything that might help him disappear."

"He never asked me about any other missions or files or anything."

"Maybe he didn't have to."

Lawson started looking all around the room trying to come to grips with everything. She so wanted Cain to be wrong but knew he probably wasn't. She had hoped that Raines' feelings for her were true but she was starting to realize that they most likely weren't.

"How often do you have your computer cleaned?" Cain asked.

"I don't know. I check it for viruses and bugs every week."

"No, I mean have the agency technician give it a complete check."

"Not in a while," Lawson replied.

"I think once we get back you should probably do that."

"You think he's got my computer hacked?" she asked, looking at her tablet.

"I think it's possible. If I was in his position, that's probably what I would do," he said.

"I would know if someone tampered with my computer."

"Would you?"

Lawson looked at him, knowing he was right again. She wouldn't have known, Raines would've been the last person she would've expected something like that from and likely would've overlooked any signs that her computer had been hacked.

"Love is blind," Cain said, trying to reassure her that it wasn't her fault.

12

On the flight back to New York, Lawson was in a very somber mood, unsettled that Raines may have been using her the entire time they were together. It was bad enough he broke up with her, then had to mourn his death, and then had to revisit everything upon learning he was actually alive. Now she was thinking that everything was a lie, and he had no feelings for her at all, which was the most upsetting, thinking she was just a pawn in whatever chess game Raines was playing.

While Lawson was having her own troubles, and not in a very talkative mood, Cain was trying to sleep on the long ride back to New York after having a brief layover in Great Britain. About an hour into the flight he had another vision. He'd seen a woman and a boy in his previous visions, in separate instances, but this one was different. In this one, the same woman and boy were together, playing together in a backyard. She was pushing him on the swing for a few moments, then waited for him to go down the slide. Just like the other visions he had, he couldn't hear any of their voices. He started moving his head around, hoping to get some clue as to who these people were. After a few minutes, Lawson could see Cain out of her peripheral vision having some type of problem. She assumed he was dreaming. She let him go for a few minutes until what appeared to be a painful expression came over his face. Lawson tapped on his shoulder to try to wake him to no avail. She then shook him more forcefully, finally able to awaken him from his sleep.

"Are you OK?" Lawson asked.

"Uh, yeah," Cain replied after taking a few seconds to get his wits about him.

"Having a bad dream?"

"No, not really."

"By the faces you were making it sure looked that way."

"No, I'm good."

Cain still seemed like he was out of it, his eyes a little glossy. Lawson kept a close eye on him for the next few minutes, unsure he was as fine as he claimed to be. He seemed like he was a little foggy to her. As the minutes went by Cain continued to shake the visions away, slowly feeling back to normal again. He looked at Lawson, wondering if he should tell her about the visions he was having. He thought if he told her then maybe she could help him in some way to figure out what was happening or who those people were. Cain knew he'd have to trust somebody eventually if he wanted help. With Lawson opening up to him about her troubles it seemed like she'd be a good candidate for him to open up to. Cain cleared his throat trying to think of a good way to talk about it.

"I, um, was wondering if I could talk to you about something," Cain said.

"Sure," Lawson replied, sensing something was bothering him.

"For the last week or so I've been having visions of people."

"What kind of visions? Of who?"

"I'm not sure. At first it was just of this woman, I don't know who she is. No voices. Just her face. Then a few days later she was walking somewhere. Then it was a boy playing on a swing. A few days after that both of them were together playing in a backyard."

"And you don't know who they are?"

"No."

"What do you think it means?" Lawson asked.

"I really don't know. Maybe I knew them before and I'm starting to remember, you know, get my memory back."

"Maybe so."

"I saw my file, but is it possible it wasn't complete?"

"In what way?"

"Maybe they're family, or friends," Cain said, hoping.

"I don't know. I saw the same file you did. All I know is that you weren't married."

"Maybe a sister."

"You're an only child," Lawson said.

Cain continued looking out the window, frustrated. Lawson could see the trying look on his face and felt bad for him. She wished she could do something for him but she didn't really know much more than what was in his file.

"Is there something that's been triggering these visions?" Lawson asked.

"No, I don't think so. Most of the time I was just sleeping."

"Maybe you should talk with a psychiatrist."

"I'm not doing that," Cain stated.

"No, listen, it might help you. Maybe he could get into your subconscious and figure things out," she said.

"I'll think about it."

"OK," Lawson said, knowing full well that he wouldn't.

"That's not all," Cain said.

"There's more?"

"I had a dream the other night that I was back in the army as a sniper."

"And?" she asked, knowing there was something he was troubled about.

"I shot someone in the head."

"Could've been something that happened while you were in the service."

"The person I shot was me."

Lawson didn't reply, not sure what to say to soothe his mind. She could see he was obviously upset by his dreams and visions but had no answers for him. She tried to calm him down.

"I know this isn't what you want to hear but it could be anything. You're trying to fit a five-letter crossword puzzle answer into a spot that's only got four spaces," Lawson said.

"What the hell is that supposed to mean?"

"That woman and boy could be anybody. Could've been an old girlfriend, a neighbor, just a friend, someone you saw on TV, maybe it's not even any of those things. Maybe it's just some woman you saw on the street and it stuck in your memory like you knew her."

Cain kept looking out the window, not wanting to hear what Lawson was telling him. She was right, but he desperately wanted it to mean something. Even if it was a little piece, at least it was a start. He stayed silent as Lawson continued talking.

"Right now, they're just visions of a woman. That's all they are. If you go around letting it eat at you like there's more to it, you're gonna drive yourself crazy. And everyone else around you."

"I don't have anyone else around me to drive crazy," Cain joked.

"OK, then me."

They dropped the subject momentarily as Lawson went back to work on her laptop. A few minutes later she still had more to say and turned it off, putting it away.

"Listen, I know you're frustrated, and I can understand. I know it's tough not knowing your past, and I can't say I know what it's like, but I am here for you. If you need help or just want to talk, don't hesitate to reach out to me."

"Thanks," Cain replied, giving her a smile.

"One more thing."

"Yes?"

"Is that woman still living in your apartment?" Lawson asked.

"You mean Heather?"

"Yeah, that's the one."

"Yeah, why?"

"It's not my business, but what is she still doing there?"

"It's not your business, but we have an arrangement," Cain said.

"She was only supposed to stay there a few days."

"So?"

"Are you two... involved?" she asked, trying to find the right words.

"She's a friend."

"People like that..." Lawson said, before being interrupted.

"She's actually a very nice person and very intelligent. You just have to get to know her. She actually has a degree you know."

"Really? That's surprising," Lawson said. "Are you hooking up?"

"That's not your concern."

"You are my concern. I'm your handler and it's my job to make sure your mind is in the right place," she said.

"Look, I kinda had an incident with the people she worked for," Cain said. "I didn't think it was wise for her to stay at her place so I told her to stay with me until she found a new apartment. They also kind of fired her so she's looking for a job."

"Like a real job?"

"Yes, a real job."

"You mean one that doesn't involve putting her ass in someone's face?" Lawson remarked.

"What is your problem with her?"

"I don't know. I know why Sanders uses her and I understand the reasoning behind it, I guess it just irks me for some reason."

"Why? Are you jealous?"

"What?!" Lawson said, her voice raising slightly. "No, I'm not jealous."

"Oh. I thought maybe you secretly wished you were in her shoes sometimes," Cain said, trying to egg her on.

"Yeah, right, don't be ridiculous."

"It just seemed like a little jealousy there."

"Listen, buster, I can get just as many men as she can if I wanted to," Lawson replied.

"Oh, I'm sure, I'm sure."

Once they arrived back at JFK airport, they grabbed their bags and started for their cars. Lawson invited Cain to her home for dinner and maybe a drink, but he thought it best to decline. He knew she was still in a highly emotional state and didn't want to complicate matters further. Besides that, he wasn't ready for any type of commitment with anyone and thought continuing any type of relationship that wasn't work related would lead in that direction. Before going home, Lawson went to the Center to drop off her computer to have it analyzed. The technician was still there as he often worked late nights and started working on it right away.

Cain walked through the door of his apartment to find it empty again. It seemed like every time he got back Heather wasn't there. He wondered where she was this time. Maybe she was out shopping again, he thought. He looked for something quick and easy to make himself for dinner and settled on macaroni and cheese. He sat down in the living room and turned on the Yankees game while he ate. As ten o'clock approached, Cain started to get concerned about Heather's whereabouts. He figured she would've been back by now. A few minutes after ten she came staggering through the door. Cain could tell right away that she was a little tipsy. He got up to make sure she didn't fall over and hurt herself. He put his arm around her shoulders and walked to the couch. By the smell of her breath she'd been drinking something fruity.

"Hey, you're back," she said.

"Yep."

"I, uh, I was gonna say something."

"You'll think of it later," Cain replied.

"You're such a cutie pie."

"Thanks."

Heather put her hand on his face and stroked his cheek. Cain sat her down on the couch and started to leave her when she grabbed his arm to sit him back down. She put her arms around his neck to move closer to him, hoping to get a kiss or two.

"You're pretty nice stuff," she said.

"You're pretty drunk," Cain responded, taking her arms off him.

"Why do you hate me?"

"I don't hate you."

"Then why won't you kiss me?" she asked, moving in on him again.

"Because I don't want to take advantage of you," he replied with a laugh.

"Please take advantage of me. I want you to take advantage of me."

"Not tonight. You need to sleep."

"What's a girl gotta do to get a kiss around here?" she stuttered.

"Be sober for one."

"And then you'll kiss me?" she asked hopefully.

"We'll see."

"Is that a promise?"

Cain laughed. "Just lay down."

"Not until you promise to kiss me."

"I promise."

"When?"

"We'll talk about it when you wake up."

"Sounds like a deal."

Cain finally eased her down on the couch, Heather falling asleep within minutes. Cain went into the bedroom for a blanket and placed it over her. He stood over her for a few minutes, watching her to make sure she was OK.

"Seems like you started a little early," Cain said to himself, looking at his watch.

Cain was pretty tired and lay down on the sofa across from her. He figured he'd stay there instead of going to bed in case Heather needed anything during the night. It was a pretty quiet night though, as Heather slept straight through to the morning. She woke up holding her head and immediately went to the bathroom. Cain heard her getting up and got up himself to make sure she was all right. A few minutes later Heather emerged from the bathroom walking a little straighter though she was still rubbing her temples trying to make the pain go away. She noticed Cain standing by the sink in the kitchen.

"Hey," she said, forgetting she saw him the previous night.

"How are you doing?" Cain asked, smiling, somewhat amused with her condition.

"My head hurts."

"I can see that."

"When'd you get back?" she asked, putting her head down on the counter.

"Oh, I rolled in last night."

"Last night? Were you here already when I got in?"

Cain laughed. "Yeah."

"Oh. I'm so sorry."

"Don't be. Happens."

"I don't remember much. I really hope I didn't make a fool of myself," Heather said.

"You were fine."

"Wait, I think I remember a little bit," she said, straining to collect her thoughts. "Were we sitting on the couch or something?"

"Yeah."

"Did I try to, uh, throw myself onto you or something?"

"Well, it wasn't quite that bad," Cain said.

"Oh God. I'm so sorry. I feel so bad."

"Heather, it's fine. You didn't do anything wrong."

"I feel like such an idiot now," she explained.

"What were you celebrating? It's not New Year's."

"A girl I used to work with at the club is getting married. She wanted to go out for drinks with some of the girls to celebrate. I didn't have anything else to do."

"Oh. Sounds nice. Did you have a good time?" Cain asked.

"Apparently I had too good of a time."

Cain laughed as he started brewing some coffee for her. As they continued talking, Cain kept making a few jokes at Heather's expense. She could tell he was enjoying her agony and seemed to be having some fun with it.

"You're enjoying this, aren't you?" she asked.

"You know, maybe a little bit."

"Glad you're getting some laughs out of my pain."

"Hey, I'm sure you'd be doing the same to me," Cain said.

"Thanks for taking care of me though," Heather said, getting serious.

"I really didn't do much. Just put you on the couch and threw a blanket on you."

"Still. It's the thought that counts."

"Well, I recall you taking care of me the night before I left. I figured it was my turn to return the favor."

They just sat and talked in the living room for a few hours, trying to take it easy. Just after twelve Cain's phone started ringing. Heather walked over to the kitchen counter to get it and looked at the screen. She made a face when she saw who it was.

"Guess who?" she asked, handing it to him.

"Hey, what's up?" Cain asked his handler.

"Just got the findings back from the technician about my computer."

"And?"

"You were right. He's been looking at my emails, case files, missions, everything," Lawson said.

"Since when?"

"For about nine months."

"So, what now?"

"I don't know."

"Can you get the IP addresses from the computers he was using to hack it?" Cain asked.

"No. He's using a very sophisticated system that encodes his info. We can see what time and general location he looked at everything, down to the city, but that's about it. We might be able to nail it down further but it'd be kind of pointless by the time we find it. He's already long gone by that point."

"What's the last few things he's been looking at?"

"You," Lawson said.

"He knew you were in Honduras before you got there. He'd already accessed your file. He was waiting for you."

"I see."

"And he knows you and I were in Indonesia. He looked at our flight information a couple days ago. Hold on," she said, looking at her phone. "Sanders is calling. I'll call you back."

"You want some aspirin?" Cain asked his hungover companion.

"Yeah, I guess I'll take some more."

Cain went to the bathroom to get some Advil for her, bringing out a couple capsules along with a drink of water. As soon as he handed Heather the glass, his phone rang again.

"Hey," Cain said.

"We have something going on. Can you come here now?" Lawson asked.

"Uh, yeah, I'll be right there."

Whatever was going on sounded like it was important

as Lawson seemed to be rushing her words. Cain quickly got his shoes on and grabbed his guns.

"What's going on?" Heather asked, concerned.

"Not sure. Have to go to the office."

"Be careful," she said, worried about the guns he was strapping on.

13

Cain rushed over to the Center, still unsure what was going on. Once he arrived he went to Lawson's office, who was waiting for him.

"C'mon, we're going to The Room," Lawson said.

"What's that?"

"It's kind of like an observation room. There's a bunch of analysts looking at information on their computers, and if there's an important mission going on, communicating with the agents in the field as things are happening."

"Oh," Cain replied as they swiftly walked.

"If we have video it's put up on the big screen for everyone to see. If there's a decision to be made then a higher up will make it... usually Sanders."

"So, what's going on now?"

"I'm still not sure myself," Lawson responded. "Sanders said he'd explain once we got there."

Five minutes later they entered The Room, Lawson swiping her ID to gain entrance. Once inside, Cain looked around the room, impressed at the sophistication of the area. There were a bunch of mini workstations, all manned by analysts on headsets, with a bunch of small TVs all over the room, with a huge screen in the middle of the wall at the front. There were a couple of supervisors going from station to station to get the latest updates that the analysts had for them. Sanders' attention kept diverting between the TVs before he realized Cain and Lawson finally arrived.

"Glad you got here so quickly," Sanders said.

"What's going on?" Lawson asked.

"Well, considering both of you have gotten involved in this I figured you'd wanna be here to see its conclusion."

"Conclusion of what?"

"We've got Raines," Sanders said.

"Where?" Lawson asked.

"He's on a plane to San Francisco. He just left Mexico an hour ago and should arrive in about two hours."

"How do you know he's on it?" Cain asked.

"We got him on video from the Mexican airport boarding a plane. We then tracked the flight information. We're tracking the flight now so we'll know when it lands."

"What is he going to San Fran for?" Lawson asked.

"Just a layover," Sanders answered. "Going to San Francisco and then Hong Kong in lieu of his final destination... Indonesia."

"He's going back," Lawson said.

"Well, we're gonna make sure he's not."

"What's the plan?" Cain asked.

"We've got two agents en route to the San Francisco

airport as we speak. They should arrive within a half hour."

"Are they capable of taking him out?" Cain asked.

"They both have considerable experience in the field. They're more than qualified," Sanders replied.

"Are they gonna kill him as soon as he steps off the plane?"

"No. As much as I'd like that it's too high profile. Our agents will be there waiting for him. They will take him into custody as soon as Raines steps off that plane."

"I thought custody wasn't sanctioned?"

"They will take him into custody and then they will immediately escort Raines into a bathroom. They will then proceed to lead him into a stall where they will promptly put two bullets in his head," Sanders explained.

"Oh."

"Then we will tamper with the surveillance footage in that time frame so there is no evidence that we were ever there."

"Sounds like it's all under control," Lawson added.

"This should be the end."

Lawson and Cain took a step back and just watched the proceedings as the time counted down. Lawson sat down in a chair and put her head down, mixed feelings running through her as she thought about what was about to happen. As much as she knew Raines deserved what he had coming to him, she still couldn't erase some of the feelings she had for him. Cain, on the other hand, was fascinated by The Room. He closely watched the analysts as they worked, magnetized by the complexity of their work. They all periodically looked up at the digital clock on the wall, anxiously waiting for that moment to arrive. As the time approached, just minutes from the expected deadly encounter, Lawson rocked on her chair, feeling like she was going to be sick.

"You all right?" Cain asked, noticing her discomfort.

"I'll be OK."

"Want some water?"

"No," she said.

Cain could see how anxious she was to the point it seemed like she might pass out. Her skin tone was getting lighter, her eyes seemed dilated, and she was heavily sweating. She was trying not to think about it but that was near impossible. Cain thought it might be best if she wasn't in the room as the incident went down to spare her feelings.

"It might be better if you weren't here," Cain said.

"I'm not leaving," Lawson replied.

"This isn't gonna do you any good."

"I wanna be here when it happens," she said, appreciative of his offer.

"Being here when it happens isn't gonna help," Cain insisted. "Your spirit isn't gonna feel lighter and angels aren't gonna come down and sing to you."

"Being in a different room not knowing what's going on isn't gonna help either. It's just something I'll have to deal with either way. I'd rather be here when it does."

Cain knew he wasn't going to win the fight, so he dropped it, hoping she knew what she was doing. Watching someone you once cared for die wasn't going to be an easy thing for her to swallow.

"All right. Here we go," Sanders said, looking at the time. The plane was due to land any minute.

They contacted their agents to check their status and

were informed that they were already in the airport, heading to Terminal 1.

"This is Langston," the agent said through his earpiece a few minutes later. "Rivers and I are in position to intercept the target."

"Good," Sanders replied. "Get it done."

The United Airlines plane finally touched down and passengers started exiting within a few minutes. The well-dressed agents stood there, waiting for Raines to show himself, prepared for a gun battle at any time if he saw fit to engage in such. Raines finally emerged, one of the last passengers to get off, and immediately noticed the two suits waiting there. He assumed they were there for him but he wasn't the sort of man who panicked at the first sign of trouble. He always calculated risks and determined when would be the right time to counteract any signs of trouble. He continued walking at a brisk pace, suitcase in hand, hoping to walk right past them. He wasn't past opening up on the two of them right there but usually was a little bit more cunning than that.

"You boys waiting for me?" Raines asked as the two men joined each of his sides, one of them grabbing his bag. They each grabbed hold of one of his arms to ensure he didn't rabbit on them. "Hope I didn't keep you waiting long," Raines joked.

"Let's go," Langston said.

"Where we going?"

"I have to go to the bathroom."

Raines knew exactly what that meant. Sanders and the rest of his crew were listening to every word on the speakers, somewhat surprised that Raines was cooperating so easily without a struggle.

"Something's wrong," Lawson blurted out, standing up.

"Everything's fine," Sanders replied, reassuring the group, though not so sure himself.

"He's going too easily. He knows there's a KOS order on him, he's seen it on my computer. He's up to something."

"Have your guard up in case he tries something," Sanders told the arresting agents.

"Roger," Langston replied.

"Maybe he just knows the game's up," Cain added.

"No," Lawson said. "That's not him. It's not in his makeup to just accept things as they are. He always has an idea to respond to a situation or an alternate way of doing things. That's just how he is. Just giving up and resigning himself to his predicament is something he's never done."

After a five-minute walk they found the bathroom. Static started blaring over the speakers in The Room.

"What's happening?" Sanders asked.

"We're losing the signal," an analyst replied.

"Why? Get it back up."

The agents and Raines walked into the bathroom and they all went to the sinks, the agents pretending to wash their hands as they waited for the bathroom to empty of witnesses. One man exited a stall, washed his hands and left, then another man finished at the urinal. As the final man left, Rivers went over to lock the door. As Rivers' back was turned to the pair, Raines produced a knife out of his sleeve, sticking it into the stomach of Langston. He grabbed Langston's gun out of his hand as Langston fell to one knee and fired two shots at Rivers as he turned around. The shots were muffled by the silencer on the gun so nobody would hear the shots and come running. Both bullets hit Rivers in his chest, instantly knocking him onto his back. Langston pulled the knife out of his stomach and got to his feet only for Raines to turn his attention to him. The first bullet entered Langston's body on the side of his head, blood splattering onto the sink and mirror. As Langston fell to the floor, Raines made sure the job was done and shot the fallen agent two more times in the chest. Langston was already dead by that point, the headshot terminating his life. Out of the corner of his eye Raines noticed the leg of Rivers moving slightly and he walked over to him. He stood over him, knowing he would perish shortly, but decided to end it quicker for him. He pointed the silencer at his head, putting one right in the center of the agent's forehead. There was no more life left within him and Raines quickly looked over his work. He grabbed the earpiece from Rivers' body and put it on. He washed the blood from his victims off his hands and quickly left the bathroom.

"Can we tap into the airport video?" Sanders asked.

"I'll get right on it," another analyst answered.

The silence was worrisome to the group, not knowing what was happening. Though they were confident of the plan succeeding, anytime something went awry that wasn't accounted for, it was a cause for concern. Lawson had sat back down with her hands together over her face, almost looking like she was praying. Cain periodically looked over to her to make sure she was OK and hadn't passed out or anything. They all anxiously waited to hear the words booming over the speakers again, hopefully that Raines had been eliminated

"Feed's up," an analyst noted as the video went up on the big screen. "That's the closest bathroom to the terminal. They gotta be in there."

Everyone intently stared at the screen as they waited for their agents to emerge. After a couple minutes of no activity they knew something was wrong.

"Something happened," Sanders said. "It doesn't take that long to put a bullet into somebody."

"Agent Langston, Agent Rivers, what is your status, over?" an analyst asked to no reply. He waited a few seconds before repeating the same question.

After a few more seconds of silence they finally heard a voice reply back.

"The target's been eliminated," the voice said.

"What took you so long?" Sanders asked, agitated.

"Just had to wait for people to clear out of the bathroom," Raines answered, hurrying out of the airport before they realized it was him.

"Where are you now? We've got video on the bathroom now."

"We already exited and are leaving the airport now."

"Well, good job," Sanders said. "We'll start erasing the evidence."

"It's been my pleasure."

Lawson suddenly stood up, alarmed at something she heard. Cain looked at her strangely, wondering if she was OK. He put his hand on her arm which she brushed off, indicating she was fine.

"It's him," she stated.

"What?" Sanders asked, turning around.

"Raines. He's alive. That's him you're talking to."

"How do you know that?"

"He said 'it's been my pleasure'."

"So?"

"Raines always said that. It was one of his quirky sayings that he liked to say," Lawson said.

"Are you positive?"

"That's him. Anytime someone said something to him that he felt like he should respond to he'd say 'my pleasure.' He's alive. Trust me."

Sanders turned back to the microphone on the desk and pushed the red button to talk.

"Raines," Sanders sternly said.

There was no reply as Sanders looked back at Lawson, who nodded that she was positive it was him. After a minute, Raines decided to respond.

"So, what tipped me off?" Raines asked.

"What happened to my men?" Sanders asked.

"I'm pretty sure you know the answer to that."

"I do."

"Shelly's there, isn't she? She has to be. She's the one who figured out it was me so quickly. Otherwise you wouldn't have known for a little while yet."

"She is," Sanders confirmed.

"May I talk to her?" Raines asked politely.

"Absolutely not."

"Tell her I'm sorry that it came to this."

"You're not one bit sorry."

"Well, that's for you to decipher. Tell her I did care for her."

"She can hear you."

"Well, it looks as though you've interrupted my plans. Now I'm gonna have to reach my destination in some other manner."

"We'll find you. Just like we did today," Sanders said.

"Even if you do, the results will play out just as they did today. You cannot out-think or outmaneuver me. I will always be one step ahead of you. So, beware of the obvious," Raines warned.

The connection cut out, ending the call, as a deafening silence permeated through the room. A look of sadness and despair overtook the faces of everyone, angry and despondent over what just occurred.

"See if you can get video of the airport and parking lots to see if we can pick up where he's at," Sanders told an analyst.

"It's unlikely we'll find him. He's probably disguised himself or laying low for a while," Lawson said.

"I agree. But let's do our due diligence, anyway."

"Well, we know he was heading back to Indonesia," Lawson said.

"Yes, but I'd say it's a good bet he'll be changing his plans now that he knows we were on him," Sanders replied. "At the very least he'll be changing his method of getting there."

"Flying's the only way of getting there."

"He knows we'll be watching the flight lists. He'll come up with something."

A few people left the room though most of the analysts stayed to continue working. Sanders huffed and sighed as he exited the room. He stopped as he reached Cain and Lawson. Lawson seemed a little dazed, stunned that what she anticipated didn't come to fruition.

"I want you two to make finding him your top priority right now," Sanders told them before leaving. "You find him. I want him dead."

14

Lawson woke up a little after five in the morning after a pretty restless sleep, nightmares continuing to run through her mind throughout the night. She dreamt of various scenarios in which Raines was killed, sometimes by her shooting him, or by Cain finishing him off. She lay in bed for ten minutes, staring up at the ceiling, wondering where Raines was at that particular time. She looked over at Cain who was still sleeping, and smiled, pulling the sheets over his naked body. After Raines eluded their capture in San Francisco, Lawson and Cain went to her house to work. Cain mainly went to make sure Lawson was OK and didn't drink herself into a stupor. He somehow managed to let her get his guard down and started drinking along with her. After a couple hours of getting their mouths wet, they repeated the steps they took in that Indonesian hotel, and had a fun-filled night of passion. She got up and took a shower, then proceeded to go to her desk, working on her computer for a bit. She felt a little more clear-headed, the lustfulness of the evening taking some stress off her shoulders.

Cain started stirring once he heard her typing away on the keyboard. He sat on the edge of the bed, yawning, and holding his head.

"Hey, sleepyhead," Lawson greeted.

"Hey."

Cain got up and dressed, wondering to himself what he was doing. He didn't necessarily regret being there, but he wasn't sure it was the right thing they should be doing. He sat down next to Lawson at her desk, looking at what she was doing. They started talking but quickly stopped when a beeping sound started coming from her computer.

"What's that?" Cain asked.

"It's an alert from the tracking program I have on there. It picked up something," she replied, looking at the information that popped up.

By the look on Lawson's face, Cain could tell it was something big. Her mouth opened the way it does when someone gets a shock that they can't believe and her eyes stared at the screen, almost like she was afraid the information would go away if she blinked.

"It's from Gutawa's computer," she said, turning to him.

"And?"

"There's an email from Raines."

It read: *Will be in Indonesia Friday. I would like to meet with you if you're available.*

Cain looked at the screen as the two of them read the

short e-mail together. There wasn't much to it or any complexities that they could see. They wondered if it was some sort of code but ultimately agreed that it wasn't. Lawson immediately called Sanders to let him know.

"Yes?" Sanders sleepily answered.

"Sorry to wake you, sir," Lawson said.

"That's all right. I was looking to get an early start this morning, anyway. I assume something's happened?"

"I just got a hit from the tracking software I put on Gutawa's computer in Indonesia," she said.

"Oh? Good news I hope?"

"I'm not sure yet. Raines just e-mailed him asking to meet with him. He said he'd be in Indonesia on Friday."

"Any reply back yet?"

"Not yet. We should look at the flight lists to see," Lawson started before Sanders interrupted her.

"There's no guarantee he's actually coming in on Friday. He might arrive Thursday. He also might not fly directly in. He could arrive via Singapore, or the Philippines, or even through Australia. Unless we have confirmed his path in, then the best course of action is to meet him there. Take Cain and go back. Get the earliest flight you can. When Gutawa meets Raines, so will you," Sanders said.

"I'll make the plans."

"Shelly."

"Yes?"

"I want you to be careful, understand?"

"I will."

"You are not an agent. I'm only telling you to go because you're directly acquainted with the way he thinks and you are probably the best person to track him. I do not want you getting engaged with him if something goes down. That's what Cain is for."

"I understand."

As soon as she got off the phone she started checking airline information and let Cain know they were flying back to Indonesia. Within a few minutes all the flight times were displayed, and she picked the one that'd get them there the fastest with the fewest layovers on the way. They wouldn't have much time to prepare as their flight would leave in six hours.

Cain immediately left to go back to his apartment. He walked in and saw Heather sleeping on the couch. A small amount of guilt slowly crept into his system for not coming home all night. He went into his bedroom and quickly packed some clothes, while also putting his guns into the secret compartment of his bag so that they'd go undetected through airport security. Heather woke up, the sounds of the drawers opening and closing waking her. She rushed into the bedroom, happy to see Cain, and hugged him. She thought she smelled a woman's perfume on him as he pulled away from her embrace.

"I was so worried," she said. "I sent you a bunch of texts but you never responded."

"Oh," Cain replied. He padded the pockets of his pants to feel where his phone was. He never even checked it once he got to Lawson's house, so he never got Heather's messages. "I, uh, forgot to check it."

"That's OK. I waited on the couch all night for you to get back. I must've fallen asleep while I was waiting."

The small amount of guilt Cain felt was growing by the moment. The fact that this woman was concerned about his whereabouts and well-being and he never bothered to even let her know where he was made him feel pretty crummy. He knew he wasn't obligated to tell her anything, but she was staying at his apartment and figured it was probably the proper thing to do.

"So, where were you?" Heather asked.

"Um, we had something important come up at the office. I just couldn't get away," he lied.

"All night? And you never checked your phone?" she asked, not quite believing his story.

"I just forgot."

A confused look came over Heather's face as she watched Cain finish packing. She wondered where he was going after rushing in from being gone all night.

"Are you going somewhere?" she asked.

He sighed. "I have to go back to Indonesia."

"Again?"

"Yeah. Looks like some unfinished business. Hopefully it won't take too long but I'm not sure."

"Oh. When's your flight?"

"A few hours," Cain answered.

"You were with someone, weren't you?" Heather finally asked, trying not to sound jealous.

"Uh," Cain mumbled, not sure what to say, and definitely not wanting to tell the truth.

"The perfume gives it away," she said.

"Oh."

"So, who's the lucky girl? Do I know her?"

Cain looked down at the floor, ashamed to look at Heather in her face. She could tell by his avoidance that it was somebody that she knew, which cut down the list of suspects dramatically. She thought for a second, then a look came over her face like she just solved a riddle. She remembered smelling that perfume before, not too long ago.

"It was Michelle, huh?" she asked.

Cain hesitated before answering, still not wanting to say. "Yeah."

"I remember that perfume. She was wearing it that night she came over here. The night we first met."

"Oh. Good memory."

"I usually don't forget things."

"I see that."

"So, are you two an item now?" she asked.

"No," Cain emphatically answered. "It just kind of happened. Nothing more than that."

They stood there in silence, both waiting for the other to continue, though neither one did. Heather knew she didn't have the right to be mad since they weren't a couple, but she couldn't help but be a little huffy. Lawson got what Heather wanted. Him. She couldn't figure out what Lawson had that she didn't. She figured she should stop peppering him with questions about it since they weren't together. He had the right to do what he wanted even though it made her heart ache. Cain could tell that Heather was a little annoyed, though he wasn't sure if it was more the fact he didn't come home or whether it was his little rendezvous with Lawson.

"Well, I should probably get going," Cain finally stated.

"OK."

"Um, I'll see you when I get back."

"Yeah," she replied, faking a smile.

"I'll let you know when I'm on my way."

Cain walked toward the door, turning around to see Heather once he reached it. He only saw her back as she was already walking into the bedroom. She had her head down and he could tell she was disappointed. Cain felt some remorse that he was the reason for her unhappiness and thought maybe he could make it up to her once he got back.

Once Cain arrived at the airport he met with Lawson, who was already waiting for him. She got there a half hour earlier and was on her computer working.

"Looks like we got some more news," Lawson said.

"About?"

"Gutawa replied to Raines' email," she said.

"What'd he say?"

"He agreed to meet with him. Ten o'clock at the Makam Perang Jakarta."

"Say that again?" Cain asked, not understanding what she just told him.

"The Jakarta War Cemetery."

"Convenient. He won't have to go far when we're done."

"I've downloaded a map of the cemetery so we can plan it out."

They looked over the plans during their long plane ride. The Jakarta War Cemetery contained the graves of almost 1,000 people, many of which died defending Java and Sumatra during the Japanese advance in 1942. Others died later in prisoner of war camps. The cemetery was in the suburb of Menteng Poeloe, almost seven miles from the center of the city. It was next to the Netherlands Field of Honour in South Jakarta. It was only open between the hours of eight and five, Monday through Friday, so

Raines obviously picked the location for its seclusion. The entrance faced the cemetery where people from the local market often blocked the access, trying to sell their wares. The cemetery was entered from the north side by a short flight of steps which led into a memorial building. Two main grass areas went through the site, one which ran north and south, the other running east to west. The Cross of Sacrifice stood in the middle of where the grass areas met. In the southern part of the cemetery lay the graves from members of India's forces. A monument was set up in this part, with sculptured wreaths bearing the words "India" and "Pakistan" beneath them. The caretakers' quarters along with a garage were also in that part of the cemetery. All graves were marked by bronze plaques and concrete pedestals. There were many sub-tropical plants, trees, and shrubs that adorned the property.

"We're gonna be met by another agent once we get there," Lawson informed Cain.

"Why?"

"To have more parts of the cemetery covered. He was doing some work in Australia, so he was fairly close to bring over."

"What's the plan?" Cain asked. "Doesn't really seem like a lot of good places to take cover here."

"The meeting's scheduled to take place at the Cross of Sacrifice. Agent Stanton will be stationed by the garage where he can see the side entrance and the Indian Forces Monument if he should go that way."

"And us?"

"We're gonna have to be at the edge of the property. There are some shrubs at the back that we can take cover in," she explained.

"I'm not really liking this."
"Why?"
"Seems too exposed."
"It'll be fine."
"We'll see."

15

Jakarta, Indonesia—It was just about ten o'clock and everyone was in position. Stanton was by the garage guarding the side entrance. Lawson and Cain were taking cover behind some shrubs near the back of the cemetery. They were lying on their stomachs as the shrubs were small and they'd be exposed if they stood up. Cain had his sniper rifle out, targeting the area by the Cross of Sacrifice. A few minutes later they saw a figure emerge, walking in the main entrance through the memorial shelter. He reached the Cross of Sacrifice and sat there, waiting for his partner.

"It's Gutawa," Cain said, seeing him clearly through the scope of his rifle.

Gutawa looked very anxious and kept looking around as he waited for Raines to arrive. He got up a few times and walked around the monument, continuing to look for him. As the minutes ticked by, Gutawa seemed like he was contemplating leaving as he walked toward the entrance a few times before circling back to his location, looking at his watch. A half hour elapsed with no sign of Raines.

"Something must be wrong," Lawson whispered.

"Maybe."

"He should've been here by now."

"Maybe he's just being extra cautious," Cain replied.

"How long should we stay here if he doesn't show?"

"We'll stay here as long as Gutawa's here. As long as he's expecting him to show then we're not bailing either."

The time slowly ticked away, Lawson repeatedly looking at her watch, anxious for her former lover to arrive. It was just about eleven o'clock when Gutawa seemed to have had enough. He started walking toward the exit when Lawson stood up. Everyone seemed to believe that Raines was blowing the meeting off.

"What're you doing?" Cain asked, trying to grab her leg.

"Let's see if he knows more," she replied as she started walking.

"No," Cain said, flailing at her leg, just touching her heel.

Cain quickly regained his position, putting the entire area within the sights of his scope. He didn't think it was a good idea for Lawson to expose herself but there wasn't much else he could do. He figured they could've tailed Gutawa to see where he went after that. Gutawa could've led them to more information that would've led to Raines in some capacity. Lawson, though, figured Gutawa knew what the meeting was about and wanted to question him about it. Gutawa stopped as he noticed a dark figure moving closer to him. He closely watched the person moving in, eagerly waiting to see who it was. He squinted his eyes trying to make out who it was. His eyes opened wider, surprised to see Lawson emerge from the darkness.

"You look surprised," Lawson said. "Expecting someone else?"

"Why are you here?"

"Same reason you are."

Gutawa shrugged as if to say he didn't know why he was there.

"It's late, it's dark, and the cemetery closed over five hours ago. I know you're not here to just walk around," Lawson said.

"I have nothing to say to you."

"I know you were here to meet Raines."

"I still have nothing to say," Gutawa said.

"You don't have to say it. I already know," Lawson said. "Raines sent you an email asking you to meet him. You agreed and set up the time and place. So here we are."

Gutawa seemed stunned that she knew the exact details. "How do you know all that?"

"We have our ways. You're not leaving here until you tell us what we want to know," she said.

"I don't know what he wanted. He said he wanted to meet, so I agreed. The purpose of this meeting was unclear to me as well."

Just as Gutawa let the words out, a shot rifled through the crisp night air. He stumbled forward onto Lawson, who struggled to keep him upright, the pair eventually falling to the ground, Gutawa on top of her. Lawson pushed his lifeless body off her and looked down at her blood-soaked shirt. She then looked over at Gutawa, who wasn't moving and appeared to be dead. Cain frantically waved his gun around, desperately trying to find his target. He was unable to do so and turned his focus to Lawson. He looked at her through his scope and noticed she was moving.

"Just stay still," Cain said through his earpiece.

"I think Gutawa's dead," Lawson replied.

"Are you hit?"

"No, I don't think so."

"Just hold on until I get you. I don't know where the shooter is so I don't know if he's got sights on you or not."

Agent Stanton left his position and came rushing up the steps to get to Lawson. Once he got there, he bent down on one knee to check her condition. As he was doing so, another shot rang out, this one ripping through Stanton's chest. The force of the bullet knocked him back, killing him almost instantly. Cain noticed the flash of the man's rifle and saw it was coming from just beyond the fence. He took off running, hoping to catch the killer before he had a chance to escape. Once Lawson saw Cain running she quickly got up and ran after him. She wasn't going to let Cain get too far ahead of her. They heard the sound of a car door shutting, then squealing away, indicating Gutawa's killer had gotten away. Cain ran to their car, refusing to let their man get away. Lawson was right on his heels and got in the passenger side.

"What about Stanton?" Cain asked.

"I think he's dead."

Cain pushed the pedal to the floor to gain speed on the fleeing suspect. He could hear the squealing of the brakes so he could tell which direction the car was traveling. The two cars zoomed through the Jakarta streets in a short pursuit that felt like it lasted a while, but only took about five minutes. The car Cain and Lawson were following ended the chase prematurely as it reached a bridge that overlooked the Ciliwung River. The car just stopped and turned completely around to face the oncoming car. Cain stopped the car about forty feet in front of the other car as they waited for the occupant to make a move.

"What's he doing?" Lawson asked.

"I don't know. You stay down," Cain said as he pulled out his Glock.

The pair sat there staring at the other car, struggling to see who was inside. A few seconds later the other car door opened, though the occupant still sat in his seat. Cain opened his door also, mimicking the other driver.

"You have your gun on you?" Cain asked.

"Yeah."

"Get it out."

Lawson took out her gun, wondering what Cain had in mind. She usually carried a gun but seldom had any use for it. The only things she ever shot at were targets on the firing range.

"If something happens to me, do whatever it takes," Cain told her.

"What?" Lawson asked, surprised to hear him talking in that manner.

"I don't know what this guy's plans are, but if I don't make it, protect yourself."

Lawson checked her gun and got it ready, anxious and nervous about what was going to happen. Suddenly the other driver got out, revealing himself.

"Raines," Lawson exclaimed.

"Yep."

"You knew it all the time?"

"I assumed so. Who else would it be?"

"Why would he shoot his own contact? He helped him disappear."

"Maybe because he found out that he talked to us. Besides, now that we know he's alive he's got no more use for Gutawa," Cain said.

"What's he doing?" Lawson asked.

Raines emerged from the car and just stood in front of it, gun in his hand, relaxed at his side. Cain and Lawson also got out, though Cain gave his partner a disapproving look, not wanting her to exit the vehicle. It was too late to argue as Cain wasn't about to take his eyes off of Raines and give him an advantage.

"It seemed as though I wasn't going to outrun you," Raines shouted. "So, stopping to face you seemed to be the proper course of action."

"You know this has to end," Cain replied.

"Does it? Why?"

"You just know it does."

"Yes, as Sanders has ordered," Raines said. "I've got no quarrel with you, Cain. We can both go our separate ways now."

"I can't do that."

"Why not? If I wanted you dead, I would've killed you in Honduras. And you know I could've. As for you, Shelly, I could've killed you in the cemetery just as easily as the others if I so desired. But my feelings for you wouldn't let me do that. I couldn't do that."

"Don't talk about your feelings for me," Lawson screamed. "You used me."

"I did. I apologize for that," Raines said. "But that

doesn't mean my feelings for you weren't true because they were. Nothing I did or have done changes that."

"What is it you want?" Cain asked.

"For us to go our separate ways. You go back to New York and I'll once again disappear," Raines offered.

"Too much has happened for us to let that happen. You've killed some of our agents," Lawson said.

"Come on, Shelly, you're much brighter than that. To just accept what you've been told. Especially by those that perpetuate the lies. I killed those who attempted to kill me, in self-defense," Raines responded. "Tell me, Cain, have you yet figured out the lies that you've been told?"

"What lies?" Cain asked.

"To which there are too numerous to respond. In time, you will figure them out as I have. I assume that you will. The facts will at some point not come together the same as they used to. The memory will come back to you and reveal the things that you've lost. You will realize that things are not as they seem. That what you've been told is not necessarily true. One day something will just seem out of place and create a domino effect in which all the pieces fall down, revealing your true self. I hope you get to that place... as I have."

"What are you talking about?"

"I wish I could tell you. But I'm afraid our time here is up," Raines said, raising his arms in an attacking stance. "We've created quite a stir and the police will be here shortly."

Raines pointed his gun at the pair, which prompted Cain and Lawson to do the same. Raines slowly started moving away from his car and toward the edge of the bridge. Cain started circling around him as Lawson stayed in her position. Raines continued backpedaling until his back hit the bridge and he had nowhere else to go.

"Well, I guess I'll see you in our next life," Raines said.

Raines fired a couple rounds in Cain's direction before quickly taking a shot at Lawson. All his shots missed as the bullets whizzed by Cain and the shot at Lawson grazed off the ground. Cain quickly regained his composure after dodging the bullets and fired at Raines. His shot hit his mark as Raines grimaced before the blow knocked him over the concrete railing. Cain and Lawson rushed over to the railing to see where Raines fell but couldn't see him in the water. Not only was it dark, but the Ciliwung River was a dirty, polluted river. Sometimes it was hard to see what was in it during the daytime. Cain put his hand on the railing as he kept looking and felt something. He pulled his hand up to see what it was and rubbed his fingers together before wiping the blood off on his pants.

"You think he's dead?" Lawson asked.

"I dunno but we gotta move," Cain replied, pushing her back to the car. "Stay here and we'll get some onlookers before you know it."

They drove back to the cemetery in the hopes of cleaning up the scene. In the event police were already there they'd keep on driving. Luckily, they had not yet arrived and Cain reached into the glove box for a spare gun.

"What are you doing?" Lawson asked.

"Fixing the mess."

Cain put the gun by Gutawa's hand and dragged Stanton's body a little to give the impression that they shot each other. He wanted to make it appear that there were no other people there and make it an open and shut case. He quickly finished his work and ran back to the car, driving back to the hotel with Lawson. Once inside their room Lawson called Sanders with an update.

"We cornered Raines on a bridge," Lawson said.

"And?"

"Cain shot him."

"Is he dead?" Sanders asked.

"I think so."

"You think?"

"The shot made him fall over the bridge and into the river," Lawson said.

"Did you see his body?"

"No. But there was blood all over the railing."

"Hmm. I'll put our sources to work to confirm it. If he's shot and bleeding he'll have to hit a doctor somewhere along the way if he's alive."

"You think he's alive?"

"Until his body is found we will go under the assumption that he is alive," Sanders said.

"Yes, sir."

"You two have done some good work on this. I want you to stay there for a few more days to see what you can find out. If his body is found it'll be all over the news."

Lawson told Cain about the instructions Sanders left for them. She could see something was wrong with him. He had this look on him that indicated something was troubling him.

"What is it?" she asked.

"It just doesn't seem right."

"What doesn't?"

"Raines is an expert shot. He fired three rounds and didn't hit either one of us," Cain said.

"Well, he was in a hurry."

"I don't think that was it."

"You think he missed on purpose?" Lawson asked incredulously.

"Maybe."

"Why would he do that?"

"You saw the result. He disappeared again," Cain said.

"You're assuming he's not dead. So, you think he staged that to disappear again?"

"Possibly. He realized he wasn't going to lose us so he set the stage at the bridge."

"That's quite a risk to take. If that's true then what would make him think you wouldn't kill him?"

"Maybe he thought it was a risk worth taking."

"No, I don't buy it. He's dead," Lawson said.

Cain continued to sit there silently, looking over to the wall. Lawson could tell something else was on his mind.

"What else?" she asked.

"I was just thinking about what else he was saying on the bridge. About all the lies."

"You don't seriously believe any of what he was saying, do you?"

"Why not?"

"He was just talking to divert our attention. Hoping to get the jump on us," Lawson said.

"I didn't get that impression."

"Trust me. I know him better than you."

"You didn't know him well enough to know he was playing you," Cain said, hoping not to offend her.

"You're right. But I do know him better than you."

"OK."

"Trust me. He knew this was the end and was just spewing crap out of his mouth trying to buy a few extra minutes to figure out his escape. We finally got him and put an end to it. This was the end," Lawson said.

"Could be. But, somehow, I doubt this is the end."

ABOUT THE AUTHOR

Mike Ryan is a USA Today Bestselling Author. He lives in Pennsylvania with his wife, and four children. He's the author of the bestselling Silencer Series, as well as many others. Visit his website at www.mikeryanbooks.com to find out more about his books, and sign up for his newsletter. You can also interact with Mike via Facebook, and Instagram.

facebook.com/mikeryanauthor
instagram.com/mikeryanauthor

ALSO BY MIKE RYAN

Book 2 in The Cain Series:

The Cain Deception

Other Books:

The Silencer Series

The Ghost Series

The Eliminator Series

The Extractor Series

The Brandon Hall Series

The Last Job

A Dangerous Man

The Crew

Printed in Great Britain
by Amazon